A FILLY
OF
OUR OWN

Richard H. Waltner

iUniverse, Inc.
Bloomington

A FILLY OF OUR OWN

iUniverse books may be ordered through booksellers or by contacting:

iUniverse
1663 Liberty Drive
Bloomington, IN 47403
www.iuniverse.com
1-800-Authors (1-800-288-4677)

ISBN: 978-1-4759-4328-3 (sc)
ISBN: 978-1-4759-4329-0 (ebk)

Printed in the United States of America

iUniverse rev. date: 08/16/2012

CONTENTS

CLINT AND LADY

Clint Haugen and his horse Lady were just a small speck on the horizon as they slowly moved northward on the vast plain between Casper and Buffalo, Wyoming Territory. Lady was getting old and Clint didn't want to push her. He was content to let her set her own pace. It seemed to Clint that he had been on the trail from Casper to Buffalo forever. There was very little change in the empty landscape. Speaking out loud he exclaimed, "Well Lady, at least we are in sight of the Bighorn Mountains so we must be making some progress."

It was spring and though the days were balmy the nights were downright cold. The first night out he huddled around a small fire fueled largely by sage brush. It burned so fast that it kept him hustling just to keep the fire going.

He thought to himself, I should have stayed in Casper a few more days, but if I don't keep moving I'll never get to Montana Territory.

Clint was an impressive figure. Six feet two inches in height and though he weighed close to 225 pounds, he was all muscle. There wasn't an ounce of fat on his lean body. His face was dark brown, tanned by the sun, a mark of so many days spent on the trail. His thick hair was also a dark brown which he wore, just to the nape of his neck; and noticeably, his cheek bones were a bit high the result of Indian ancestry in his family history. He was dressed in jeans, cotton flannel shirt, boots and a low, flat crowned hat with a medium sized brim. He was a handsome man, in a rugged sort of way.

Woman were attracted to him not only because of his appearance but because of his demeanor as well. He was a kind, considerate and compassionate man, hardly the qualities one would expect to find in a man who was perhaps the fastest gun in the territory.

Around his waist he wore a pistol belt with cartridges. In his holster was tucked a Colt 45 that was one of a kind. He wore it in such a way that suggested gunfighter. In addition, a rifle scabbard was attached to his saddle containing a 44-40 Winchester Model 1873 lever action rifle, He had drawn his pistol on a challenger only once. He did not kill the man and that bothered him. He did exactly what Ben had warned him not to do.

"If you must draw your pistol Clint, shoot your adversary; If you don't and it becomes a habit you will get yourself killed."

For a moment he was ready to kill the man, but Val pleaded with him not to. His adversary's pistol hadn't cleared leather before the barrel of Clint's Colt was aimed squarely between his eyes. He begged Clint not to kill him and had it not been for Val he would have done just that, or so he thought.

"Lady, I can only hope that when the time comes I will not hesitate to shoot."

The last thing Clint wanted was a reputation like Ben's. Ben told him that after his first kill word got out about his fast draw and after that he didn't have a peaceful moment. He was forever being challenged by practiced gunmen and by shave tails who had no business challenging anyone to a draw. It was only after he went into seclusion down the road a couple of houses from Clint's that a kind of peace settled over him.

Speaking out loud he said, "Maybe I should put Ben's gun in my saddle bag and carry dad's Colt. With it on my side I would look more like an ordinary cowboy." Arguing with himself he continued, "But why have such a beautiful revolver if I'm not going to carry it? It will stay where it is, in it's holster. If the time comes when I need to switch guns I'll do it."

Clint and Lady had been on the trail from Santa Fe, off and on for about a year and a half. He was slowly working his way northward. His goal was Montana Territory and he was anxious to get there.

Lady was not a big horse, but she was strong and Clint was an easy load for her. They loved each other. The two had been companions for better than seven years. Together they went through wind and rain, sleet and snow, burning hot and freezing cold temperatures. As much as possible when it was cold they tried to keep each other warm. Clint had a horse blanket tied to his saddle that he draped over his legs and Lady, when the thermometer plunged. When it got too cold they holed up in a town if they were lucky enough to be close to one. When the sun was too hot Clint and Lady traveled by night. If they were near a stream with a clump of trees, that's where they holed up for the day.

He had stopped a number of times to take on odd jobs. At one time he helped with branding calves, another he worked in a mine, something he hated since he experienced mild claustrophobia. He took on the jobs largely to keep in shape physically.

Clint was born on a very hot summer night in July. His mother suffered greatly through the birth and she never failed to remind him of this on his birthdays. Clint was going on 24. His father, who had been a deputy sheriff in Santa Fe, was shot in the back and killed by a drunken drifter and he was raised primarily by his mother. He remembered only a little about him. When he was killed his mother was left without any source for money and went to work doing anything she could find. She was not a big woman, in fact she was small and petite, a very pretty young woman.

Her jobs were often more than she could handle. Because of this, she aged rapidly. She was only 37 when she died; Clint was 13 at the time.

Because of the love he had for his mother, he had developed a strong affinity towards women and became their protector.

From time to time he and Lady would lie up in a town to get supplies, especially food and ammunition for his Colt. He practiced his fast draw daily which required plenty of ammunition. Ben had told him, "Take it from me Clint, one can get rusty in a hurry."

After bathing in streams and stagnant ponds, he looked forward to a hot bath. The break also gave him and Lady a chance to rest.

Wherever Clint went his pistol went with him; Ben had told him he most likely had the fastest draw in the West. He never knew when he might be challenged to a gun fight.

LIZ

One of the towns at which Clint stopped was Pueblo. His hotel was directly across the tracks from a saloon and bordello. He seldom heard the word bordello used, it was always whore house.

One evening he crossed the tracks from his hotel and went into a saloon for a drink or two. He sat by himself, preferring to be alone. He wasn't exactly anti-social, but neither was he overly sociable. He thought that maybe this was due in part to the fact he and Lady always traveled alone. In addition he had grown up with very few friends.

He was sipping his drink when he heard a woman scream. He jumped to his feet, turned towards where the scream was coming from and saw a man beating on a young woman. The girl was holding her arms and hands in front of her face trying to protect herself from the man's blows.

He rained blow after blow on her arms and hands. There were many men in the saloon, but no one moved to rescue her.

In Clint's haste to get to her, he overturned his table. He grabbed the man, lifted him over his shoulders and threw him against an empty table.

In a second he was on him. He hit him in the face once, then twice. His blows were not enough to render the man unconscious. Clint said, "Apologize to her or the next blow will knock you across the room."

The room became silent as Clint drug him over to the girl. With his hand on the collar of the man's jacket, he held him up in front of her and with a voice seething with anger said, "Apologize to her and be damn quick about it."

"Like hell I will, she's nothing but a cheap whore."

Clint spun him around and hit him hard in the face.

"Apologize to her or when I get through with you, you'll be unrecognizable."

The man looked up and when he saw Clint's face his eyes opened wide.

"OK, OK, I'll apologize. I'm sorry I hit you Liz, I guess I just lost my cool."

"Now," said Clint, "apologize for calling her a cheap whore."

"I'm sorry I called you a whore Liz, I hope you'll forgive me."

With that said, Clint let the man go. He heard someone say, "Did you see his eyes, they looked like the gates of hell."

"Yeah, and did you notice how he wears his gun, I've got a hunch he knows how to use it."

Clint turned and faced the patrons seated at the tables. No one moved. In a voice still laced with anger he said, "Do you men just sit idly by while a defenseless girl is being beaten? Not a one of you moved to help her. I'm not a violent man, actually I'm a God fearing, peace loving man, but no one and I mean no one strikes a woman in my presence and get's away with it. I don't care what she is, being a prostitute makes her no less a woman."

Then he turned to the girl. "Liz, that's your name right?"

"Yes it is," the girl answered."

"Would you join me at my table for a drink?"

"You heard what the man said, I'm a whore. Do you want to buy a drink for a whore?"

"I sure do, I've got a table, let's go to it."

The table was still on it's side. Clint grabbed it and set it upright. His glass was broken and his drink splattered over the floor.

"Bartender, bring me a bucket and a rag and I'll clean up this mess and bring us two drinks. Liz what will you have?"

"Just a small glass of Brandy."

"I'll have another whiskey."

"May I ask you your name."

"It's Clint."

"Thanks Clint. There are men who will beat on a woman just because she's a woman. I can't recall anything I said or did to cause that bum to become so violent. A few minutes ago he was up in my room with me and seemed to be perfectly happy. He wanted me to drink whiskey with him. I said I wouldn't because I hate the stuff. Then he started hitting me."

"Are you hurt?"

"My arms are bruised a bit, but nothing serious."

"How old are you Liz?"

"I'm 19."

"Nineteen?" He said with surprise.

"I know Clint, I'm still a girl."

"How long have you been a prostitute?"

"Six months."

"How did you ever happen to get into such an awful business like this?"

"I was on my way to Kansas City. The train had a two hour lay over while taking on water so I went to this saloon across the tracks to see if I could get a bottle of sarsaparilla. Mabel, the Madam of the place, sat down with me and asked if I wanted a job as a bar maid. All I would have to do was see to it that the men had their drinks and be sociable with them. She said I could leave any time I wanted. I thought it would give me a flavor of the wild west. I agreed and that was the biggest mistake I made in my life. You won't believe this Clint, but I haven't been outside this building in six months. I never was a bar maid who just circulated among the men. Mabel told me I was going to be a prostitute and if I gave her any argument or attempted to escape she would beat the hell out of me. Clint, I was a virgin when I prostituted myself for the first time. The guy was filthy, hadn't bathed or washed his hair in weeks and he reeked of alcohol. It was horrible."

"I can't believe that Liz, you are literally a prisoner in this damn hole."

"I am Clint. I live in constant fear."

"How about the other girls?"

"We are all young and were lured into prostitution by the same kind of promise Mabel made me. Because we're young, men have to pay a premium for us."

"How much does a customer have to pay to spend time with you.?"

"Seven fifty. The going price in the other saloons is five dollars."

"And how much do you get from the seven fifty?"

"All we get is fifty cents and that has to be used to pay for our room and board. So we get nothing."

"What? You have to pay room and board? You aren't being truthful with me are you Liz?"

"I am Clint, every word of it is true. Do you see why even if we could escape we have no money for a train or stage ticket out of here."

"What about your family, do they know what you are doing?"

"Heavens no. Mabel forces us to write home every month telling our families that we have work as clerks in a general merchandise store or whatever and how much we like it. Of course our letters go through her first."

Clint was silent and just shook his head.

"Liz, I'm going to get you out of here and out of town."

"Even if you could, I have no money, where could I go?"

Pointing to the bar Liz said, "Do you see those two big men, at about the center of the bar? One is wearing a tan hat and the other a black hat."

"What about them?"

"They're on Mabel's payroll to make sure none of us tries to flee."

"How many girls are here?"

"Four of us. There is Jolene, Frieda, Kathy and myself. We are all about the same age."

"Once you're out of this hell hole, where would you like to go Liz, back home or on to Kansas City?"

"If I could get away from here I would go back home. I'm only 19 Clint and already my life has no meaning to me."

"And where is that?"

"California."

"Do you have a lot of personal belongings in your room?"

"No, nothing worth while."

"You're leaving here Liz and you're going back to California. Do you know when the next train going south comes through here?"

"The day after tomorrow." Pausing she added, "Clint, we'll never get by those two brutes. I've seen them in action. When they fight they leave their opponent half dead. One is called Bull and the other Bear and as you can see, for good reason."

Mabel marched to the table and in a snappy and commanding voice said, "Liz, what the hell are you doing sitting around shooting the bull with this cowboy? You have customers waiting."

Liz cowered.

"Liz is through with your damn business Mabel. She's leaving with me, now."

"Sure she is sonny, that will be the day."

"From what Liz has told me you are a cheap, mean old bitch and I might add, not worth a damn cent. The guts of you keeping the girls here against their will. It wasn't so long ago that we fought a war to do away with slavery. Your girls are slaves woman. You should be behind bars."

Clint stood, all 6'2" of him. Mabel looked at him and blinked.

"Now old hag, sonny is taking Liz with him."

"Like hell you are."

Mabel turned and called, "Bear, Bull, there's trouble over here."

The two men walked over to Clint's table.

"What's the problem Mabel?"

"This guy thinks he's going to take Liz with him."

"Oh he does, does he. OK mister, get up and get the hell out of here."

"I'm already up and no one tells me to get out of anywhere."

Clint had sized up the two men. They were as big as he, but he stood three to four inches above them.

"Come on Liz, let's go."

One of the men looked at Clint for a moment, his face changed expression then he swung at Clint. Clint threw up his left arm and the intended blow glanced off it. He drove his right fist into the man's mid section, with his left he hit him full in the face knocking him over the empty table next to them.

The second man had worked his way behind Clint, grabbed his arms and held on tight immobilizing them for a moment. Clint bent over suddenly with the man hanging onto him. He went flying over Clint's back and landed hard on the floor. Clint was on him before he was able to stand. Grabbing him by the front of his jacket he jerked him to his feet he pounded him again and again in his face. With a hard right hand blow to the man's chin he sent him sprawling. When he hit the floor he didn't move. The first man was trying to rise. In a moment Clint was on him.

"Enough, enough," the man cried out.

"Help your partner up and the two of you sit down at that table right behind you."

Clint snatched their pistols from their holsters and placed them on the bar some distance away. He walked back to his table, turned to Mabel, and said, "If you weren't a woman I'd beat you half to death. Truth of the matter is I don't consider you a woman, but rather a mean spirited old hag. I won't strike you, but I sure as hell would like to. Now sit down and don't say a word or I'll forget you are a woman."

Turning to Liz who was staring at his face with eyes wide open, he said, "What's wrong Liz?"

"Your face Clint, for a moment it was the face of a wild man."

"I've been told something happens to my appearance when I get enraged and I'm afraid I was enraged." Then he hollered out, "If there's anyone in here who wants to pick up where these two clowns left off, show yourself, now."

No one moved.

"If any of you are thinking about gun play, think again. The two men I just beat on will live another day, but if I have to draw my pistol you're dead."

Again no one moved. Then Clint turned to face Mabel.

"You bitch, you lousy bitch enslaving the girls and keeping them locked up. I'd like to give you a beating like I did your two stooges. Liz, run upstairs and see if any of the other girls would like to leave this hell hole with you. There's no time for them to grab their belongings, just tell them to bring themselves."

Mabel started to talk, "You can't—"

"Shut up bitch, not another word out of you."

Again the expression on Clint's face began to change. He could tell by the fear written across Mabel's face. In just a few moments all four girls came running out of their rooms. Customers stepped out of the rooms yelling, "Come back, come back, I wasn't finished, I wasn't finished."

"Go across the tracks to the hotel girls, I'll be there in a moment. Now I don't know where you men stand on what I've just done. This damnable Mabel kept the girls in literal slavery, something I'm sure you didn't know. There are other brothel's in town besides Mabel's that are available to you. Now, get back to your drinks and don't anyone try anything foolish."

Clint reached down and tipped his holster just a bit forward.

"Mister," one man said, "None of us in here likes Mabel, we liked her girls, but not Mabel. You won't get any trouble from us."

"I'm sorry all this had to take place, but for me there was no alternative. After what I just did, I know you won't believe it, but let me say it again, I'm a peace loving man. When I see a woman being abused, I forget I'm a man and become like a ferocious animal. Keep that in mind."

"Yeah, we saw it in your face," replied one man.

Clint picked up his hat, set it on his head and said, "Good night gents. As for you Mabel, I hope you have a hell of a night and when the word gets around, I hope to hell you will soon be out of business."

As Clint left one of the men turned to his partners at the table and said, "If I hadn't seen it I wouldn't have believed it. Did you see his face. It almost didn't look human."

Clint found the girls standing by the desk. He spoke to the clerk, "Do you have one big room that the girls will fit into?"

"I've got one room with two double beds."

"Is that OK with you girls?"

"That's wonderful Clint," Liz replied.

The clerk gave a key to Liz and the four girls went to their room. Clint stayed behind.

"I'd like a room and right next to theirs if you have one."

"There is one, Mr., Mr.—"

"Just call me Clint. If anyone comes in here looking for the girls or just snooping around, you come and tell me pronto."

"I'll do that Clint."

Clint paid for the rooms then went to his. As soon as he heard the girls moving about he knocked on their door.

"Girls, it's Clint."

He heard the door being unlocked and then Liz opened it. He stepped inside and found all four in various stages of undress.

"Come on in Clint. We're all about ready to take a bath," said Liz.

"The water's almost hot."

"Darn it Liz," he replied, "You should have told me."

The girls all laughed.

"Of course Clint," Liz said, "No man has ever seen us with our clothes off."

Laughing Clint replied, "I guess you're right Liz. Now let's get down to business. A train going south is due in town day after tomorrow. Where would each of you like to go?"

"Clint, as I told you in the saloon, none of us has any money."

"Don't you worry about that, just let me know where you want to go."

Each girl told him where she would like to go.

"I'll get tickets for you in the morning and soon you'll be out of here. Keep your door locked. I'll be close by if you need me."

Clint went back to his room, retrieved one of the bags that Ben had given him and counted out several gold coins. The next morning he went to the depot and purchased four tickets.

"Of course the girls will have to make changes along the way."

"I'm sure they are aware of that. One is going to California, one to Oregon, and two to Texas."

The station agent gave Clint his change. He counted it and said, "I'll be darned, there's almost enough here to get the girls home. Tell me, how did you know the tickets were for girls?"

"You're Clint, right? What you did last night is all over town. You did a very noble thing by freeing those girls. We knew they were being held against their wills but the sheriff we have is worthless. He wouldn't do anything about it. The people of Pueblo are going to try hard to see that Mabel's den of iniquity will be closed forever."

"Don't you think they should all be shut down?"

"I'm afraid that wouldn't work. Men are men, you know."

"I guess you're right."

"Tell the girls I've written on the back of each ticket where they'll have to make changes."

Clint went back to the hotel and gave each girl her ticket and enough money to get them home.

Looking at him with a smile and moist eyes Liz said, "We'd like to pay you back Clint, but we have only one thing to offer and it's yours if you want it."

Clint broke out laughing and said, "Darn it girls, I'm not going to say I wouldn't like to take you up on your offer, but I'm going to decline it."

When the train arrived Clint escorted the girls to the depot. There was a one hour wait as the engine took on water. Clint stayed with the girls.

He was pacing back and forth when Liz came up to him and asked, "Are you nervous, Clint?"

"Yes Liz and I'll be nervous till you're on the train and on your way. There are people in this town who don't like me."

"Would you mind telling me where you're headed to?"

"Montana Territory."

"I wish I were going with you."

"Not really."

"I guess not, I'm anxious to get home."

The conductor called, "All aboard."

The girls left the depot. Each one gave Clint a hug and thanked him again for what he was doing. Liz was the last.

"Clint, what if you had picked a different saloon to visit? This wouldn't be happening."

"It was meant to be Liz"

"May I give you a kiss?"

"You sure can."

And they kissed.

"Whew," said Liz, "It's been a long time since I kissed a clean cut, handsome man who knows how to kiss." Smiling she added, "Are you sure you don't want to take me up on my offer?"

"Darn it Liz, you don't know how much I'd like to, but, but,"

Liz broke in, "You're concerned that I might not be clean, right?"

"I'm not going to lie to you Liz. Yes, I'm concerned. You told me how filthy was the first man you had sex with. I'm sure there were many that way.

Promise me you'll see a doctor as soon as you get home."

"The very first thing Clint. How come we couldn't have met earlier under different circumstances? You are such a polite, considerate and caring man, and I might add darn handsome as well."

"You can drop the handsome Liz. I guess that kind of meeting just wasn't meant to be. I want you to know you are a very attractive girl. You make my heart beat faster. I'm so darn glad we got you out of that hell hole before it made an old woman of you prematurely."

"One more question Clint, but first of all, I wouldn't even consider dropping the handsome bit."

"What is it Liz?"

"What happens to your face when you get angry?"

"I don't know Liz, I've never seen it. All I can tell you is that I have an affinity for women which I'm sure comes from the love I had for my mother. When I see a woman being abused I get livid with rage. I guess I see just a bit of my mother in every woman and it's as if it's my mother who is being beaten. That's the closest I can get to an explanation."

"You almost killed three men defending me."

"Not quite."

"All aboard:"

"Goodbye Liz. Now remember, be a good girl."

Liz laughed and replied, "Come on Clint, I know how to make lots of money and I'm darn good at it. You think I'm going to pass that by?"

"LIZ."

Laughing, Liz said, "I can't have my virginity restored, but I promise you one thing Clint, the next man I make love to is going to be a man I love. Good bye Clint."

Early The next morning, Clint and Lady were already miles north of Pueblo. He said to Lady, "Liz is such an attractive girl Lady. We met then we parted, like two ships passing in the night. You know Lady, I think I could have fallen in love with her. Lady, I'm a man and I need a woman. Darn it, right now I don't feel much like one. Liz offered herself to me and I turned her down. Well, there wouldn't have been time for us to pair off anyway."

"We have a little less money now, but I think Ben would have approved of how it was spent. We still have a long ways to go. I hope we can get as far as Cheyenne before we have to hole up for the winter. We can't attempt to cross Wyoming during the winter months. I've been told it has awful winters with a lot of cold, snow and wind. We could die in something like that."

Clint stopped briefly in Colorado Springs to replenish supplies. He made inquiry as to the wisdom of moving on to Denver and was told that ordinarily he would have a couple of weeks before the snow would start flying.

"We usually have a storm, sometimes a pretty heavy one, then things calm down for a few weeks before winter really picks up steam."

"Well Lady, it's on to Denver and hopefully from there to Cheyenne. It would be great if we could get that far before winter sets in."

In Denver he was told that if he was lucky, he would have a week or two before the weather got really bad.

"You might have to spend a cold day and night or two on the trail, but with any luck at all you should be able to make it to Cheyenne."

"We'll chance it Lady. We've spent cold and snowy days on the trail before, once or twice more isn't going to stop us."

Fortunately the snow and cold waited until they were just outside of Cheyenne. They literally came in on the wings of a storm. The first thing Clint did was find a stable for Lady. He stopped at the first one he saw which was pretty well on the south end of town and visited with the owner of the stable. He found him a congenial and friendly man. He wanted to know where Clint came from.

"Many places I guess, but Lady and I started out from Santa Fe."

"That's a long way off. When did you start north?"

"About a year and a half ago."

"What, and it's taken you that long to get to Cheyenne?"

Clint told him about the jobs he worked on the way, about frequent stops for supplies and about his concern with pushing Lady too hard.

"You must think a lot of that horse?"

"She is my best friend and companion and we have been through hell together. Lady is old and I'm not going to push her. She sets the pace and not I. Now tell me, will she get good care here? Most likely she and I will stick around until spring or at least until it's safe to be on the trail again."

"I can promise you Mr., Mr.—"

"Just call me Clint, and what's your name? I guess we should know each other's name since we will be seeing a lot of each other the next few months."

"My name is Andrew, but friends call me Andy. I prefer you use that moniker rather than Andrew. That's far too formal." Extending his hand to Clint he continued, "I'm glad to meet you Clint and welcome to Cheyenne."

"Thank you Andy. I'll be in about every day just to let Lady know I'm around. Now that she's taken care of I need to look after myself. Would you tell me where I could find a room for the next few months?"

"Sure can. On your way into town you passed the Golden Slipper Saloon. Go straight east from there and three houses down you'll find a house with a sign in front advertising rooms for rent. Fran should have a room or two available. Fran is a good Christian lady Clint, good to visit with and a darn good cook. I've heard her rooms are clean and cozy."

"Is it possible for me to store my saddle here Andy?"

"Sure thing, you don't want to be dragging that with you everywhere you go."

As Clint was removing Lady's saddle Andy noticed the size of Clint's saddle bags.

"I usually don't see such big saddle bags. What are you carrying?"

"Grub, clothing, a blanket for Lady, a change of clothes, ammunition, things like that. Remember we are on a long trip with a lot of empty space between towns. I had the bags specially made for me."

Clint thought to himself, I can hardly tell him there's gold and Ben's pistol in the bags as well as food, a change of clothes and other items. Would it be OK with you Andy if I paid you by the month?"

"You can pay me by the week if that would suit you better."

"I'd rather pay you by the month. How much is it for keeping and feeding Lady?"

"Fifty dollars a month."

"Fair enough Andy." Reaching into his pocket Clint came out with a $50.00 gold piece.

"I don't see much gold or silver anymore, seems many folks have switched to paper money."

Smiling Clint said, "Well Andy, if you'd rather, I'll go to the bank and exchange this gold for paper."

"No way Clint, I prefer gold to paper any day."

Clint gabbed his saddle bags and rifle and started out the door of the livery stable.

"See you tomorrow Andy."

"Well," he said to himself, "so far so good. Now if Fran has a room for me and will feed me I guess I'm set for the winter."

He found Fran's house right where Andy said it would be. When he knocked on the door a pleasant looking woman, who he guessed to be in her late 50s, early 60s answered.

"I assume you're Fran. Would you have a room for me, a room I can rent for the winter months?"

"I sure do, and if you're interested you can also eat breakfast and your evening meal here."

"I'll take the room and accept your offer to feed me. What do you charge for the room and the meals?"

"The room will cost you five dollars a week and the meals another ten Dollars; fifteen dollars in all. And let me say, I'm a very good cook.

"That sounds fair to me Fran. May I call you Fran?"

"You sure can. And what should I call you?"

"My name is Clint Haugen and you just call me Clint."

"Come on in Clint and I'll show you to your room. I'll be serving supper in another hour. I'll expect you to join us. Oh, by the way, would you mind leaving your revolver in your room while you're in the house?"

"Of course not Fran, so long as you're other boarders leave their guns in their rooms."

"If they argue with me, they don't stay here."

"Good for you."

Andy was right, the room Fran gave him was comfortable and his first meal at her house was excellent. When they finished eating Clint said to Fran, "Fran, I want you to know that's the first really good meal I've had since leaving Santa Fe, and that's been a long time ago."

Three other men ate their evening meal at Fran's. One spoke up, "I'm Cliff. So you're from Santa Fe. It's been years since I last visited that town. I suppose it's growing like all these western towns."

"I'm Clint, and yes Cliff, Santa Fe is growing. I've been in the Springs and Denver, seemed to me they're getting to be pretty big towns."

"Just like Santa Fe and Cheyenne, they're growing, growing too fast to suit me. Where're you heading to Clint?"

"Montana Territory."

"I'm afraid you're going to have quite a wait before you can start out again. There's a lot of open country between here and the Territory and you don't want to get caught out in it when one of our rip, roaring storms hit. I'll tell you one thing Clint, you won't feel crowded in Montana Territory."

"That suits me fine Cliff and for your open spaces and winter storms, I want nothing to do with them. That's why I'm here."

"In the morning Clint took $75.00 out of his saddle bag and gave it to Fran.

"I've got some paper money here Fran, will you take it?"

"Of course Clint. Whenever I get paid I march right over to the bank and deposit it. It makes no difference if it's gold, silver or paper."

"Is it OK if I pay you once a month?"

"Actually Clint, I prefer once a month to once a week."

"Fran, I'm not a drinking man, that is not a heavy drinker, though I like a drink now and then. Can you recommend a saloon that's nice and quiet and where men behave themselves?"

"You came by the one I would recommend Clint. It's called The Silver Slipper Saloon. It's owned by a young woman who recently inherited it from her father. There are girls available there; they are available in all the saloons here in Cheyenne. Val doesn't tolerate drunkenness or rowdiness in her saloon.

She has a couple of big fellows who see to that, she calls them bouncers. If someone gets out of hand those two fellows bounce him right out the front door."

After breakfast, Clint's first stop was at the bank. The bank only had a few customers when he walked in. He waited for a teller and when one was free, asked if he could see the bank president or someone pretty high up.

"Sure thing young fellow, let me get Mr. Hawkins."

In a minute a nice looking man dressed in a suit came around the teller's counter and introduced himself. Clint likewise introduced himself then Mr. Hawkins asked, "Is there some reason you want to visit with me?"

"Yes sir, and could we do it in private?"

"Follow me into my office."

When they were seated, Mr. Hawkins asked, "Now young man, what can I do for you?"

"Mr. Hawkins, I have quite a bit of money in my saddle bags, too much to be lying around during the next few months. I would like to deposit it in your bank."

"Just how much money do you have Clint?"

"I don't rightly know, Mr. Hawkins. You see I've never counted it."

"Never counted it?"

"Let me explain."

Clint proceeded to tell Mr. Hawkins about his long relationship with Ben and that just before his death, Ben had given him the money since he had no kin to leave it to.

"I really saw no need to count it. When I needed a little I just reached into one of the bags and took it out."

"He must have been a generous man."

"He was, believe me and the best friend I could have had. He was like a father to me"

"Tell you what Clint, I'll have one of our tellers count it so we know just how much money we're talking about here."

"I'd appreciate that Mr. Hawkins."

A teller came into Hawkins office and took Clint's saddle bags and disappeared into another room. He was gone for some time during which Clint and Mr. Hawkins visited. Clint gave him a short overview of his life since he was a small boy. When he finished the teller returned with Clint's saddle bags and gave Hawkins a piece of paper, then he left the office.

"My gosh Clint, have you any idea just how much money Ben left you?

In gold, silver and paper money, he left you close to $15,000."

Clint sat in dazed silence.

"Fifteen thousand dollars, are you sure? You mean I've been carrying $15,000. around with me for a year and a half? The Good Lord sure was with me, why I could have lost the bags, someone could have stolen them or someone could even have killed me if he knew how much money was in those bags."

"And you never counted the money?"

"Never did. I never saw any reason to put what I thought was maybe One or two thousand dollars in a bank account. Had I only known. Well, I guess money is just not that important to me."

"Now that you know how much you have, how are you going to use it?"

Clint was silent, then a smile lit up his face.

"Well," he said, "Now the possibility of buying property for a small ranch in Montana Territory becomes even more real to me."

"That would be a good investment Mr. Haugen."

"Please, call me Clint. How do we go about this deposit business?"

"We open an account in your name and give you a receipt for the amount deposited. Your money isn't put into the bank's vault, the bank invests it and you get interest on the principal amount you deposited.

Right now railroad stock is a good investment especially as the railroad extends into smaller towns. You know Clint, you may very well be leaving Cheyenne with more money than when you arrived. Keep enough money for the next month; then when you need more, come to us and make a withdrawal. When you are ready to leave Cheyenne, I will give you a Banker's Check for the amount in your account. You can deposit the check in a bank near to where you settle in Montana. A bank check is a very safe way of traveling with your money since you and only you can cash it or deposit it."

"You mean I won't have my gold and silver?"

"Well, if you want your money in gold and silver, yes you can, but would that be wise?"

"I guess not, but I want to take some out in gold and silver as a remembrance of Ben."

"There's nothing wrong with that, Clint; you just decide how much gold and silver you want and it will be yours."

"That sounds very good, Mr. Hawkins; that's the way we'll do it."

"Now we have some papers for you to fill out; then we'll give you an account number and a deposit slip for the amount in your account."

When Clint was ready to leave, he extended his hand to Mr. Hawkins and said, "I guess now I can breathe easier."

"You sure can Clint. You made a wise decision and thanks for choosing our bank to do business with. Stop in from time to time so we can visit."

Time seemed to drag by for Clint. He stopped in at the stable every day just to let Lady know he was still around. It was obvious to him that Andy was taking good care of lady.

It was several weeks later when he first visited the Silver Slipper Saloon.

As was his habit, he sat away from where most of the patrons were sitting.

Fran was sure right, the saloon was quiet; and in the time he was there no one caused any trouble. After his initial visit he would go to the Saloon at least once a week. He never stayed long since just sitting and doing nothing soon became boring. Girls were available, attractive girls, but his fear of catching a disease kept him away from them. Not once did they solicit him.

Darn it, I don't know how much longer I can go without a girl, he thought.

It wasn't long before Fran and Clint became friends. Fran invited Clint to use her sitting room anytime he wanted. Her husband had left her with a library of considerable size. There were a few books that caught his attention.

On Christmas Eve, Fran invited him to attend church with her. He accepted her invitation. Year's ago Clint's mother had made sure that he accompanied her to church on Christmas Eve. Fran fixed a large Christmas dinner with all the trimmings. It revived memories of the Christmases he and his mother spent together. The difference was that they never had a table loaded like Fran's.

New Year's Eve was one time when the Silver Slipper pulled out all the stops and liquor flowed freely, however, the celebrating was not allowed to get out of hand.

Like December, January passed slowly. Clint was getting restless, he was anxious to be on his way.

"Well Lady," he said on one visit, "We still have February, March and part of April to struggle through before we can be on our way."

VAL

It was mid February and Clint was making his weekly visit to the Silver Slipper Saloon. While he was sitting at what had become to him his table, an attractive young woman approached him.

"My name is Valerie Noble, the owner of the Silver Slipper. Do you mind if I join you?"

"Of course not."

Clint stood and helped seat Valerie. She looked up at him, surprise showing on her face.

"Well thank you; I didn't think men did that any more."

"This is one man that does Miss? Mrs.? My mother saw to it that I learned some manners."

"Miss is correct, please call me Val. I returned from the east in time for our New Year's celebration. Since then I've noticed you come to the saloon about once a week, have your drink and then leave. You're always alone. Is there some reason for that?"

"You're right, I'm always alone. I'm not the most sociable kind of guy. Actually, I rather prefer being alone."

"I'm sorry," Val said, "I'll leave."

"No, no, please don't leave, I'm talking about men not women." Clint blushed. "Darn it, that didn't come out right. Let me explain. I'm holed up in Cheyenne for the winter months. As soon as weather permits I'll be leaving. Further, I don't mind telling you that men who spend most of their time in a saloon are not my kind of people. That doesn't sound right either, does it?"

Val laughed and said, "I think I know what you mean Mr., Mr.—"

"It's Clinton, Clinton Haugen, but please call me Clint."

"I'm glad to make your acquaintence Clint. You say you're holed up here in Cheyenne for the winter months?"

"Yes I am, I'll be on my way as soon as the weather is decent enough to allow me to go north."

"Do you have a particular place in mind?"

"I can't be specific, but yes, my destination is Montana Territory."

"Where are you from Clint"

"I guess it's correct to say Santa Fe, however lately, as a result of my northward trek I'm also from many places."

"I'm afraid I don't understand."

"I guess I have a way of saying things that don't make much sense.

Lady, my horse, and I, have been on the trail from Santa Fe going on two years now. We spent some time in several places; but our starting place was Santa Fe, where I was born and grew up. Does that make sense?"

"It makes perfect sense."

"I'd like to compliment you on your Saloon, Val; it's quiet in here, no loud piano pounding away and no girls sitting on my lap trying to coax me to go upstairs with them."

"Thanks Clint. There should be one saloon in Cheyenne that is quiet enough for a person to do some serious thinking. As you have observed, I do have girls, but the men who want them know they're here. They don't have to solicit. In fact I forbid it. Have you been in any of the other saloons?"

"No I haven't and I have no intention of visiting others. Tell me Val, starting when I was back in Santa Fe, I was told that Cheyenne was a magnet for fast draw artists. Is that true?"

"I'm afraid it is Clint. If you want to go looking for them, you'll find them. I'm concerned that one day one will sneak in here and the reputation of the Silver Slipper as a nice quiet and safe place to play cards and drink and visit the girls will be over." Val was quiet for a moment then asked quizzically, "Since you asked, are you by any chance a gun fighter?"

Clint smiled and replied, "Do I look like one Val?"

"I saw you come in. You move like one, but no, you certainly don't look like one."

Clint thought, I'm going to have a little fun with her.

"Tell me Val, what does a gun fighter look like?"

"Well, he, he, I, I—" Val burst out laughing. "To be truthful, I haven't the slightest idea since they all look different. You set me up for that, didn't you?"

"I cannot tell a lie Val. I sure did."

Clint and Val soon became good friends. Whenever Clint came in for a drink Val joined him. It wasn't long before he knew her background and she his. Their friendship also made the time pass faster for Clint.

February and March went by and April was upon them. Almost every day Clint found himself ready to take a chance with the elements; but each time he did a storm set in and he thanked his lucky stars he didn't set out for points further north in Wyoming. What added to his urgency was the realization that he and Val were falling in love and if it were to be expressed openly leaving her would be all the more difficult.

One evening Val said to him, "Clint, have you ever given any thought to settling in Cheyenne?"

Clint was quiet. He looked at Val and a weak smile formed on his face.

He thought, here we are falling in love and we can't express it much less show it to each other.

"No Val I haven't. Cheyenne is not my kind of town, and this is not my kind of country. My destination is Montana and that's where I intend to end up."

"There's nothing to hold you here?"

Well, he thought, I have to be honest with her.

"Yes, you Val. Our relationship is now more than mere friendship. I've fallen in love with you, but it can't be. This is your life. You wouldn't come with me to Montana, and I couldn't live here. I'd be like an unpicked wild berry dying on the vine.

"We'd make a good pair Clint."

"Now be honest Val, are you willing to Leave Cheyenne and The Silver Slipper? Are you willing to climb onto a horse taking only a very few of your belongings with you and head to Montana Territory with me? Lady and I have encountered about every kind of weather nature can hand out. Would you be willing to share that with me? I've had to go as long as a week without a bath because we couldn't find a pool of water or a stream. The sun has both baked and froze my face. There are times when even I wonder if I'm doing the right thing."

"I couldn't, Clint. I've been brought up with a silver spoon in my mouth. I couldn't survive a week out on the trail."

"I'm just so darn glad that we me met Val. Initially I don't think either of us gave thought that we would fall in live."

"So am I, Clint. I'm really going to miss you when you leave. I've looked so forward to your daily visit's these past months. Look about you, those are the kind of men I'm going to have to contend myself with once you leave."

Clint reached across the table and put his hand over Val's.

"I'm going to miss you more than you can know. Once again Lady and I are going to be all alone on the trail. I know that just thinking about you will make the loneliness more tolerable."

"Some where along the trail you're going to find a girl who will fit right into your groove, and she's going to be one lucky girl."

"I'm beginning to wonder if that will ever happen. First there was Liz and now you. Especiallyl you Val, Liz and I really didn't know each other well enough to go beyond much more than friendship."

"It will happen, Clint."

The middle of April finally arrived and Clint made ready to leave. He closed out his account at the bank. He took $500. out in Gold and silver and $250. In paper money. The balance was in the form of a bank check. And Mr. Hawkins was right. He withdrew almost as much as he had deposited. His money couldn't have been invested more wisely. He also settled up with both Andy and Fran. He said his goodbyes and was ready to leave.

For the last time he went to see Val at the Silver Slipper. He dreaded saying goodbye to her. He asked himself, how does one avoid falling in love with such an attractive and intelligent girl? There is no way we could make it work; our worlds are much too different.

He and Val were visiting when Clint had to go out back to answer nature's call. When he returned, he quietly stepped inside and instantly froze. In the short time he was gone a gunman had come into the saloon and was holding up the place. He was up at the bar, his left arm around Val's neck and his right hand holding his gun pressed against her head.

"Barkeep, give me all the money you have behind the counter. You card playing, drinking gents empty your pockets. Anyone who holds back gets a bullet in the head. If you try any tricks this lady gets a bullet in her head. Now, be quick about it. When I'm finished, if anyone asks you who robbed you, tell them it was Kid Zoro, the fastest gun in Cheyenne."

Clint silently stepped back outside and ran around to the front. The door was open. The two men who were supposed to be guarding the guns were no where in sight.

"My number's 36," he said to himself. "I have to find my pistol." It took him just a moment to locate peg number 36. Quickly he strapped on his pistol, adjusted it to the way he liked it and then stepped into the saloon.

The man was still going from table to table dragging Val with him and collecting money. With a voice filled with anger Clint said, "OK fast gun Zoro, stop hiding behind a woman's skirt and prove to me that you're fast."

"Clint," Val screamed, "No, don't, you're no match for this man."

"Well Sonny Boy, I'm afraid you just signed your death warrant."

"You know big mouth, you're the second one who has called me Sonny Boy and I don't like it. You've got a big mouth, but I don't think you're as fast as you think you are."

Zoro went for his gun. It wasn't half way out of it's holster when the barrel of Clint's Colt was staring him in the face. With a voice that sent a chill down Val's back Clint said, "Now big mouth, say your prayers, your time has come." Clint raised his gun so the sights fell directly between Zoro's eyes when Val screamed, "Clint don't, please don't. He's no longer a threat to you or any of us. If you shoot him now it would be equivalent to murder and you couldn't live with that."

Zoro was blubbering, "Don't shoot; please don't shoot. I give up. You're a hell of a lot faster than I am."

Val could see tension go out of Clint's shoulders. Slowly he relaxed.

"Someone run and get the sheriff. All right you, let your gun fall back into its holster. Now with two fingers grab the butt, slowly draw it out and lay it on the table in front of you. One false move and you're dead."

Zoro did as Clint told him.

"Now step back from the table. Further, further I said."

"I'm going, I'm going."

Clint stepped forward, took Zoro's gun off the table and stuck it through his belt. Then he holstered his own gun. He walked over to him and shouted in his face, "You lousy scum, you're so damn brave that you have to use a woman as a shield. Apologize to her and be damn quick about it."

"Zoro was looking at Clint's face as was Val. Wide eyed Zoro turned to Val and said, "I apologize woman, I apologize."

Then Clint hit him hard square on the jaw. Zoro slid across the table behind him and lay still.

"Clint stepped up to Val and said, "Are you OK? He didn't hurt you, did he?"

"I'm OK Clint, how about you? Your face, your face—."

"I know Val, the face of a wild man. It gets that way when a woman is abused in my presence. Val, I must tell you goodbye now."

"Can't you wait Clint?"

"No, Val, I must leave now." He put his hands on Val's shoulders, looked her in the eyes and said, "Val, I didn't lie to you. I never have. I'm not a gun fighter. I'm fast on the draw, it's something Ben taught me, but this is the first time I've had to draw my gun on a challenger. I didn't shoot him Val."

"Clint, I, I—."

"Don't say it Val, you know I feel the same way; but it would never work out. It's so good we met each other and fell in love even though we didn't expect to. Good-bye Val."

"Clint, why do you have to leave now, so sudden like?"

"As soon as word gets out about my fast draw every gun fighter in town will be out looking for me and I don't want it to spill over into The Silver Slipper Saloon."

"Will I ever see you again Clint?"

"I don't think I'll be coming back this way, but who knows what fate has in store for us? Goodbye, Val, please take care of yourself."

Clint pulled Val close and kissed her, kissed her hard. She returned his kiss with equal vigor.

"Good-bye, Clint and thank you for coming to my rescue. As painful as this good-bye is, though it was short, I'm so glad we met. I'm so glad our relationship developed into love for each other. Please take care of yourself Clint. I will remember you always."

"I won't forget you Val, the thoughts of you will make my days on the trail less lonely, and Val, if anyone comes in here looking for me tell them I headed south."

Clint kissed Val softly this time then in a moment he was out of the door and gone.

First he ran to Fran's boarding house, grabbed his saddle bags, bedroll and rifle, and yelled his goodbye to her as he ran down the steps. Fran yelled, "Clint are you leaving now, so sudden like?"

"I am Fran, Val will tell you why. Take care of yourself. You've been like a mother to me these past few months."

He got to Andy's livery stable as quickly as he could, saddled Lady, said his goodbye once more to Andy and turned to leave.

"Clint, why so quick?"

"Val will tell you Andy. Thanks for taking such good care of Lady. If anyone comes looking for me tell them I headed south."

As he started out of the stable, Andy called out, "Be careful Clint, don't get caught in a spring blizzard."

For ten minutes Lady ran hard then Clint slowed her down.

"Enough running, Lady, I don't think anyone will be on our trail this soon. Darn, I didn't want to leave so fast; I wanted to spend more time saying goodbye to Val."

A bit further on he said to Lady, "Lady old friend, I guess I never will find a girl for myself."

There wasn't much daylight left, however, in order to put as much distance between himself and Cheyenne as quickly as possible, he decided to ride all night. There was about a half moon in the sky making enough light to see the stage coach trail between Cheyenne and Douglas. Lady was more than rested up and he believed he could stay awake till morning.

Though the night was cold, it wasn't as bad as Clint thought it would be. The air was calm which made it more comfortable. He was able to stay awake until morning and once the sun had warmed the air he pulled off the trail, found a wooded cleft between two hills and slept.

He awoke when Lady nudged him. He looked up at the sun and said, "Thanks Lady, it's past time we hit the trail."

The day went by without incidence. The sky was clear and the sun bright which made for a balmy day. Lady set her pace and Clint stayed with it. By the end of the day Clint believed they had made at least 30 miles.

"Two more days and we should be past Douglas, Lady, then it's on to Casper."

Eager to get to Casper, Clint stopped only for the nights and for water for Lady. He kept his canteens full. It was five days after leaving Cheyenne that he finally reached Casper and just in time. A spring storm hit the area and he had to hole up for three days.

I should take this opportunity to rest up, but I'm too darn jumpy. I need to be on my way.

Once the storm passed and the temperature warmed, he and Lady set out once again for the long ride between Casper and Buffalo."

"There's nothing in between but open prairies, Lady; it will be a long lonely ride, but once we hit Buffalo and if Andy is right, we should run into rolling hills. Two days out from Buffalo we should be close to Sheridan.

From Sheridan it's only a short distance to the Montana border. We'll take a break in Sheridan, I think we will have earned a day or two off the trail.

One thing about our slow pace, it sure gives me a lot of time to remember and to reminisce."

"Lady, did I ever tell you that mother was a devoutly religious woman?

The day before the man who killed dad was hanged, she seemed to be nervous, jumpy and a bit out of sorts. I could tell something was bothering her, she was not her usual self. Finally, turning to me she said, 'Clint, 'Get your jacket, We're going to the jail' I asked; 'Why mother?' 'You'll see when we get there.' Taking me with her we went to the jail. When the jailer gave her permission, she marched back to the killer's cell. Scowling, he looked at her and said, 'What do you want woman?' Mother looked at him with kindness in her face and with a soft and steady voice; replied, 'I'm the wife of the deputy you murdered.' Mother was silent for a moment, then continued, 'Tomorrow you are going to meet your maker. I just want you to know that I forgive you for killing my husband.' With that she turned and we left the jail. I don't know if that made an impression on the condemned man or not. I asked mother, 'Why did you tell him you forgive him?' 'Because it was the Christian thing to do.' After that mother's disposition changed back to the way it was before we went to the jail. He killed my dad, mother lost her husband and yet she could tell him she forgave him."

"I believe the things mother believed in, Lady, but I'm afraid not with her fervor. Although forgiving the man was the Christian thing to do, I don't believe I could have done it. I was too young to really comprehend what was going on. From a little tyke on mother had me on my knees as she prayed. I try to believe like mother, but I just can't be like her. There are people I don't like, but I don't hate anyone though I come darn close to it when I see a woman being abused."

"You know Lady, I don't know if I remember the detalis because I was there or if mother told me about it so often that I have just added it to my store of memories. I'm sure glad you're a good listener Lady, I get tired of riding in silence. And why not talk rather than just thinking about it."

CLARENCE

Clint and Lady were somewhere between Casper and Buffalo, when something caused Clint to look behind him. A man with rifle in hand was riding hard in his direction. He stopped and waited. When he pulled up beside him, Clint could see he was unshaven and grizzled looking.

Clint guessed him to be about 60 yeas old. Holding his rifle on Clint he said, "Unbuckle your pistol belt and throw it on the ground."

Clint replied, "No, that's something I'm not going to do. This Colt was given to me by a dear friend who told me to take very good care of it.

Throwing it on the ground certainly wouldn't be giving it much care."

For a moment the man was stumped "Damn it, don't you realize I could shoot you out of your saddle."

"Why, just because I won't throw my pistol on the ground?"

"You must be one of those cattle rustling bums. I've lost over two dozen head in the last month."

"Now tell me, do I look like a cattle rustler? Where are the cows I rustled?"

"Well, darn it, you're trespassing on my property."

"If I am, I'm sorry. I'm trying to follow a straight line between Casper and Buffalo."

"Is that where you're heading, Buffalo?"

"No, actually I'm on my way to Montana Territory."

"You certainly look decent enough. What's your name young fellow?"

"Clint, Clint Haugen."

"Where are you from?"

"SantaFe."

"Golly sakes, you're a long way from home. You know, Clint; it's just plain hot sitting out here in the sun. What say we mossey over to those cottonwood trees down by the creek and get out of the sun. By the way Clint, my name is Clarence Fogert."

"Clint reached over and took Clarence's extended hand.

"I'm glad to meet you Clarence. I'm surprised how few people I've seen since leaving Cheyenne."

"There's not many folks out this way. As you've noticed, the ranches are far, few and in between."

When they reached the trees they dismounted and led their horses to the shade.

"Got anything to eat Clint?"

"I've got some jerky, some cheese and a bit of crusty bread. Seems that's all I've been dining on since leaving Cheyenne."

"I'll tell you what. My Mrs. packed me a couple of beef sandwiches.

I'd like you to have one."

"Thank you Clarence, but I can't eat your lunch, I'll make out."

Pushing a sandwich toward Clint, Clarence said, "I insist. Clint I've been admiring that Colt of yours. Mind if I see it up close?"

"Not at all, Clarence."

Clint pulled the thong off the hammer, gently lifted the pistol from it's holster, opened the gate, held it skyward, slowly turned the cylinder and let the cartridges fall into his hand. Then handed it to Clarence.

"Don't you trust me, Clint?"

"Of course I do Clarence. The man who gave me this pistol gave me some very good advice. He said that if anyone wants to see your pistol, take out the cartridges first."

"Very good advice, but there's one flaw in it. Let's say the guy who wants to see it waits until it's unloaded, pulls his gun, holds it on you and rides away with your fancy pistol?"

"You're right Clarence, you're so right. That could be a very bad mistake."

Clarence examined the engraved and gold inlaid Colt carefully, gave a low whistle then handed it back to Clint who immediately reloaded it and tucked it into it's holster.

"That's a beautiful and very expensive pistol Clint, how in the world did you ever get ahold of it?"

"I got it from a very dear friend. You may not believe this Clarence, but Ben was a gun fighter, one of the few that survived."

"A gunfighter and he gave you his fancy pistol?"

"Yes Clarence, when he gave it to me he was a worn out old man.

Well, I guess he wasn't that old, but he sure looked old. His gun fighting days were over."

"That's interesting. Tell me about him Clint."

"It's kind of a long story, you sure you want to hear it?"

"I sure do."

BEN

"Dad was a deputy sheriff in Santa Fe. One day a drunken drifter shot him in the back and killed him. I was just a kid then about five years old I would guess. I really never got to know my dad, Clarence, he wasn't home much and then he was taken from mother and I. After dad died, mom decided to stay in Santa Fe and work at odd jobs."

"Two houses down from ours was one that was vacant, and had been for several months. One day on my way home from school, when walking by the house, I noticed this old man sitting in a chair on the porch. I greeted him, and he just ignored me. When I told mom about him, she told me that the Christian thing to do was to be friendly toward him even if he was unfriendly. I guess I was about 10 years old then."

"So, every time I walked by the house and he was on the porch, I greeted him. He never said anything. One day when I walked past his house I went up to his gate and was going to talk to him. He took one look at me and said, 'Get the hell out of here, kid; and leave me alone.'

When I told mom about his outburst, she said, 'Just continue to be kind to him.' I did and it paid off. One day I went up to his gate again. He looked at me with anger in his eyes so I asked him, 'Why do you dislike me?' He was quiet and then said, 'I don't dislike you kid, open the gate and come on in.' I sat down beside him. He wanted to know my name. I told him and then asked for his name. He said, 'I don't give my name out to anyone.' I asked him if I could call him Ben. He chuckled and said, 'if you'd like, sure, call me Ben.'"

"Well Ben and I became good friends, real good friends. Truth be known, he was like a father to me. When mom baked bread or rolls, I always took him some of whatever mom had baked. Mom said I should invite him for supper. Believe it or not he accepted. He was a perfect gentleman with mom. Said thank you and no thank you, things like that. After that first invite he had supper with us many times. Often he gave me a $20.00 gold piece to give to mom for food."

"When mom died about two years after Ben moved into his house, it broke me all up. I was alone or so I thought but I had Ben. Dad had no kin Near-bye and neither did mother. I took odd jobs, like sweeping the floors in the hotel rooms, emptying chamber pots, things like that. I didn't make much money. Well, one doesn't remain a kid for very long. As I grew older, our friendship only deepened."

"When I was about 15 or 16, I had to spend more time looking after Ben. Seems he always had a twenty dollar gold piece in his pocket. He would give it to me to buy food or whatever else we needed. Ben was going down hill. I saw to it that he always had food and a bottle of whiskey. He liked a drink now and then, but I never did see him drunk. He once told me that too much whiskey affected the brain, which would slow his fast draw. During the summer months I chopped a lot of wood to keep Ben warm during the winter months."

"We were visiting one evening when Ben said, 'Clint I haven't much longer to live. Would you see to it that I get a decent burial?' I said,' of course I will Ben.' Then he said, 'I have something for you.' He reached behind his chair and came out with a small bundle in his hand. Now I'm serious when I say this, Clarence. Very lovingly he unwrapped what ever it was he had in the towel. When he finished, there it was, the most beautiful Colt revolver I had ever seen. I remember saying, 'Oh my goodness Ben, what a beautiful revolver you have.' 'Not I Clint, it is now yours. I said, 'Ben, I can't take it from you.' 'Oh yes you have to, I have no one else to give it to. Now take it Clint, it's yours. Guard it with your life.

It's one of a kind and I'm going to teach you how to use it.' And he did.

We went to his back yard so no one would see us and I practiced and practiced and practiced, day after day, drawing that beautiful gun from it's holster. Ben told me I had to keep practicing until he said I was ready, then it would be time to quit. It was awhile before he said, 'Clint now you're ready. You're faster with that pistol than I ever was. Let me give you a bit of advice. Never draw it unless you really have to, but if you have to, use it.'"

"Ben hadn't been on his porch for two days. I was worried. I knew something was wrong. I entered his house and called out his name. I heard a faint response and found Ben on the floor in front of his easy chair. I quickly dropped on my knees by his side. 'Ben, what's wrong?' Ben lifted his hand and put it on my arm. He gazed up at me and said, 'My time has come Clint, I'm dying.'"

"I asked him, 'How long have you been on the floor?' 'Since last evening. I was hoping you would come looking for me. Go in the kitchen and on the top shelf of the cupboard you will find several cast iron pots. Take them out and you will see two leather bags. Bring them to me and hurry.' I got the bags and brought them to Ben. He asked me to open them. Inside was some money. I asked Ben if he had also been a bank robber. He forced a smile and replied, 'That's something I never did Clint. The money represents some winnings at gambling and some of it I got from fast guns that challenged me. I figured since they were trying to kill me the spoils were mine. It's yours now Clint, I will have no use for it where I'm going. Spend it frugally and it should last you long enough to find a job that will sustain you.' Hesitatingly I said to him 'I can't take your money Ben.' 'There is no else for me to leave it too.' Then he repeated himself. 'As I told you Clint, where I'm going I'll have no use for it.' I asked him 'where is it you are you going Ben?' He answered, 'Some place where we are going to meet again, Clint.' 'What was that?' I asked. He repeated, 'Some place where we will meet again. 'I didn't know you had religion. Awww, Ben, I'm so glad.' 'I didn't till I met your mother. While you were in school she would come visit me often. Your mother was a very persuasive and persistent woman Clint. I looked forward to her visits. Like you are, she was a very intelligent, perceptive, and loving woman. We talked about many things. You and your mother embraced me as one of your own and I became one of the family. The two of you were the only family I really ever had; and I came to love both of you. I didn't know what love was, but when I got that warm feeling inside toward the two of you, I knew. I'm sorry your mother had to leave you so soon and sorry that I have to leave you now, but my time has come.' I asked him, 'What am I going to do Ben, I'll be all alone?' His reply was, 'You'll do just fine Clint, I have no doubt about that.'"

"Ben groaned and put his hand on his chest. 'Clint, lean closer to me I can't talk very loud. You're a good young man, one of the best. Your mother did a wonderful job of raising you. You are honest, careing and compassionate. You took an old gun slinger under your wing and helped put meaning back into his life these past few years. Never change Clint, never change. Promise me you will never change, both for your mother's and my sake. There are too few like you.'"

"I knew Ben was breathing his last. He whispered to me, 'Clint, I want you to put my real name on my grave marker.' 'What is it Ben?' He replied, 'Raif Sampson. Quite a name isn't it?' I asked him if it would be OK if I put Raif (Ben) Sampson on the marker. 'That would be fine, son. Let me repeat one more thing Clint, Don't draw your gun unless you absolutely have to. The one thing you don't want to do is establish a reputation for if you do, you will live out your life in misery.' Then Ben stopped breathing. I wept bitterly. Everyone I loved had died. First dad then mother and now Ben. I do believe I knew what mother felt when dad was killed. I really was alone in the world."

Clint stopped talking lowered his head and bit his lower lip to keep the tears from coming. In spite of his effort not to do so, the tears came.

Clarence remained silent. Then Clint looked up at him with tears in his eyes.

"I'm sorry Clarence, I didn't mean to do that."

"Don't apologize Clint, you've had a lot of unhappiness in your short Life."

Clint continued, "I made burial arrangements for Ben and saw to it that the name Reif (Ben) Carlson was inscribed on his grave marker. After Ben's death I stayed around Santa Fe for a few years. I decided there was nothing in Santa Fe for me. It was then I started moving north. I've been on the trail right at two years Clarence."

"Clint, would you answer a question for me?"

"Sure, what is it?"

"Have you ever had to draw your pistol against a challenger?"

"Yes I have Clarence. In fact it wasn't very long ago, it was back in Cheyenne. I was so much faster than he that I didn't have to shoot. Ben said that if I had to draw shoot, however a very attractive young woman stopped me from doing so. I was angry, very angry, but now I'm so glad I listened to Val. I left Cheyenne in a hurry. I didn't want word to get out that I had out drawn Kid Zoro until I was down the trail a good distance from Cheyenne."

Clarence was quiet. Then said slowly, "Clint, let me give you a bit of advice. When you are threatened with death by some gun slinger, don't make a habit of pulling your gun and not using it. If you continue to do that the time will come when unless you shoot, your opponent will kill you.

Ben knew what he was talking about. This may not be the wild west as it once was, but it sure isn't tamed yet."

"I've thought about that Clarence, but how does one prepare oneself to take a man's life"?

"I don't have an answer for you Clint, but somehow you're going to have t do it. Let me give you another word of advice if you'll take it. Do you have another pistol?"

"Yes, I have dad's Colt and the one I took from the gun slinger in Cheyenne and this beautiful Colt Ben gave me."

"Wear one of them Clint. Some one is going to bushwhack you just to get your fancy pistol."

"Your right Clarence. I'm sure green for being 23 years old. I guess I have a lot to learn."

"Can you draw your dad's six gun as fast as your fancy one?"

"Not quite, but plenty fast enough."

Clint got up, walked to his saddle bag and came back with his Dad's Colt which was wrapped in the same towel in which Ben's fancy pistol was when Ben gave it to him. He took off Ben's pistol belt and replaced it with his dad's, walked about ten feet from where he and Clarence were sitting, set up 5 stones, stepped back, turned and fast as lightening drew and fired 5 quick shots sending all five stones flying.

Clarence whistled. "My gosh man, you are a fast gun, you must do a lot of practicing. I didn't even see you going for your pistol."

"Yes Clarence, I'm a fast gun, a very fast gun. And yes, I practice a bit every day. I keep a good supply of ammunition in my saddle bag."

"By golly Clint, you blew all five of those stones sky high. You're not only fast but accurate as well."

"It does no good to be fast if you can't hit your target."

"You're sure right about that. Clint, I sure hope you never have to draw to kill. If you do and word gets out, every so called fast gun out here will be looking for you."

"I know, that's why I left Cheyenne in such a hurry. I'm learning that being a fast gun can be both a blessing and a curse."

"That's a good way of putting it. One question Clint. You set up only five stones, why not six? After all, that cylinder holds six rounds."

"Let me show you Clarence."

Clint drew his gun, emptied the cylinder, cocked it and turned it so Clarence could see it from the side.

"Look at the hammer Clarence. As you well know, that thing sticking out is the firing pin. If I put in six rounds, the hammer would be resting on a live cartridge. Should I drop it and it landed on the hammer, I could kill myself or some innocent bystander. It's darn good advice from Ben. The first time I shot his Colt, I loaded all six chambers. Ben said, 'Whoa there, you load it with five rounds not six. The firing pin always rests on an empty chamber.' Now that's not the way he actually told me.

Those words came out between all kind of cursing."

"Damn good advice Clint."

Clarence looked toward the sun and said, "Why don't you set up camp for the night right here Clint. It won't be too long before evening sets in."

"I appreciate that very much Clarence."

Both stood, Clint extended his hand and Clarence took it. It was a friendly clasp.

"You're about 25 miles from Buffalo and another 40 miles to Sheridan.

You've got several days to Sheridan and then another good day of riding to the Montana border, so you have about a week of riding ahead of you Clint. I must be going, Martha will be wondering where I am."

"Thank you for your hospitality, Clarence, I am most appreciative."

"Certainly had you pegged wrong Clint; you're one nice guy. Can I give you just one more bit of advice?"

"Go right ahead."

"Find yourself a pretty girl, marry her and settle down. Wyoming and Montana have a lot of pretty girls and many of them are a real catch.

And Clint, keep that fast gun of yours in it's holster as long as you can."

"Thank you for your advice Clarence, I'm very glad to have met you."

"Me too Clint."

The next day Clint rode as far as Buffalo. He saw no one on the trail.

"You know, girl," he said to Lady, "If I didn't have you to talk to, I do believe I'd forget how to talk. We've been traveling all day and haven't seen a soul. This sure is empty and monotonous country. But I'll say one thing, the Bighorns to the west sure are a pretty range of mountains."

Clint found a small grove of trees next to a small stream. That's where he and Lady spent the night.

"Lady, we're about two miles from Buffalo. I don't think I'll start a fire this evening. Something tells me it wouldn't be a wise thing to do. Clarence said there were some land problems up this way and I sure don't want to get involved."

The next morning Clint got an early start.

"Well Lady, about two more days and we should hit Sheridan. I'm sure glad to leave that flat, country we just came through. The hills up ahead look mighty good after the dessert. I like this country. Maybe I'll just stick around here for awhile."

As he rode along he could see a few ranch buildings. In the evening as he pulled the saddle off Lady he said, "Well lady, I figure about 15 or 20 more miles and we should be in Sheridan. I guess we don't have to start too early in the morning."

TESS

After a breakfast of jerky and a piece of dry bread, Clint and Lady started out for Sheridan.

"I'll tell you one thing, Lady, when we get to Sheridan I'm going to eat a horse. Excuse me Lady, I mean a steer. You're lucky you have food all around you."

Clint had been following a ridge line. Up high he and Lady had not come across any water.

"We're getting some water for you Lady, and I should fill my canteens."

They rode over a hill and stretched before them was a beautiful green valley.

"Look at that Lady, isn't that a sight to behold. There should be plenty of water down there."

As Clint descended west into the valley, he rode over a hill and ahead of him was a fairly large house with a few out buildings.

"There's a windmill Lady, we should be able to get some water."

As he approached the house he saw no sign of life.

"I wonder if anyone lives here, lady? Sure doesn't look that way. Well, I'll just go up to the door. Maybe the folks are inside. You know Lady, I think it's about time I put dad's Colt in my holster. We're no longer alone."

Clint rode up to the front door. He was about to dismount when the door suddenly opened and a young woman stepped out holding a rifle in her hands aimed directly at him.

"Good morning ma'am. I just stopped by to see if my horse and I could get a drink of water from your tank."

"I'll bet you want a drink of water. Get off my place, you're trespassing."

"Sorry ma'am, I don't mean to trespass, but my horse and I need a drink of water. Especially Lady here. She's had no water since early morning."

"There's no doubt in my mind that you're one of Carter's men looking over my place."

"Who's Carter?"

"Don't act dumb, he's the one you take orders from."

"Ma'am, I don't know any Carter and I don't take orders from anyone. I'm on my way to Sheridan and all I want is a drink of water for my horse and me. And would you mind pointing that rifle some place else. It's making me nervous. My name is Clint, Clint Haugen. Five days ago I started out from Casper on my way to Montana Territory. Actually, I started out from Santa Fe. It seems like months and months ago. It appears you aren't going let Lady and I get water from your tank so we'll be moseying along and hope to find someone who is more hospitable."

"You know ma'am, you could learn a few manners. Do you aim your rifle at every stranger that comes to your door? It's obvious you don't give a stranger a drink of water either."

Clint turned Lady around and started towards the north.

"Wait a minute, get your drink and then get off my place."

"Thank you ma'am, much obliged."

As Lady was drinking from the tank, Clint said, "You know Lady, that young woman sure is pretty and she seemed to be mighty scared. I wonder if she's alone or has a husband around somewhere. One thing is certain, she certainly isn't friendly. Lady, I think it's time to be on our way."

Clint had just climbed into the saddle when he heard hoof beats rapidly approaching.

"They sure seem to be in a hurry. Something tells me to stick around here a little while."

Clint was to the side of the house where he could not be seen. He worked his way directly to the north of the porch. This gave him a partial view without being seen.

Four men on horseback were approaching and soon were close to the front door of the house. Again the young woman stepped outside with the rifle in her hands.

"I know you, you're Carter's men. Get off my place. You're trespassing and there's a law against it."

"What law, there's no law out here? The boys and I were on our way to Sheridan to have a little fun with the girl's at Evonne's Bordello. Then we remembered you were here. We decided why should we pay for sex when we can get it here for free. You're prettier than Evonne's girls anyway. To make it easy on yourself just be nice and cooperative other wise we're going to have to rough you up a bit. Which will it be?"

"You come one step closer and I'll kill you."

"Have you ever killed a man Tess? I don't think so. If you shoot me there are three men who will fill you so full of lead it will take a horse to drag you off your porch."

"That would be preferable to what you men plan to do to me. You men will all be charged with rape," she said tearfully.

"Don't be silly girl, now put down that rifle and be a good girl."

He sprang forward, grabbed the rifle by the barrel and twisted it out of the girl's hands and threw it aside.

"Well, I see this isn't going to be easy."

He swung his left hand and hit her hard on the side of the face. She fell back against the cabin. Next he grabbed her by the shoulders.

Clint stepped from behind the corner, his face filled with anger. He let out a yell that scared the hell out of the men.

"Get your filthy hands off her, now;" He looked at the three men who were still on their horses.

"You men put your hands on the saddle horn and keep them where I can see them." The men obeyed.

The man who hit the girl said, "Mr., I don't know who you are, but you just signed your death warrant."

"Seems to me I heard that before."

Clint turned slightly and faced the man. Looking him in the eyes he said, "Are you sure you want to draw on me?"

The man looked at Clint, the angle at which he carried his gun and slowly moved his hand away from from the butt of his gun. In a moment Clint was on him. He hit him and hit him hard. The man hit the ground.

"No one hit's a woman and threatens her with rape when I'm around."

Clint threw a quick glance at the three mounted men.

"Keep those hands on the saddle horn."

He reached down, grabbed the spokesman by the front of his jacket And hit him again, hard. He hit the ground like he had been pole axed.

"Alright you three, get down off your horses, throw this damn woman beater over his saddle, tie his hands and feet together and get the hell out of here and be damn quick about it."

"Yeah, yeah sure, we don't want any trouble with you," replied one of the men.

The men quickly turned their horses and rode off in the direction from which they had come. The girl was still on the floor leaning against the cabin pressing the back of her hand to her bleeding mouth. Clint got her to her feet and helped her to a nearby chair.

"Tess, I guess that's what that S.O.B. called you, if I were you I'd pack a few things and leave the place. I have a hunch those bums will be back.

Thank you for the water, Lady and I'll be on our way."

Tess who hadn't yet spoken a word said, "No, no please don't go. I'm sorry, I thought you were one of them."

"I tried to tell you otherwise."

"I know, but I was too frightened to really listen to what you said. I, I, don't know if you're interested, but I just took a pie out of the oven before Carter's men rode up. Come on in, I'll make a pot of coffee. It's noon and I'm sure you're hungry."

"That sounds real good ma'am."

"You heard right, my name is Tess, Tess Hawks. It's really Theresa, but I prefer being called Tess."

"And mine is Clint, Clint Haugen."

"Thank you Clint. You saved me from an awful fate and most likely my life."

"Can you make it into the house?"

"I think so. It looks like he cut my lower lip pretty badly."

"Here, let me see."

Clint pulled her lower lip down." "It's cut alright, but not too bad. It's going to hurt for awhile."

"The pain is nothing compared to what they were going to do to me. I knew that sooner or later Carter was going to send some of his men to rape me, but I never thought there would be four of them."

When they were in the cabin Tess said, "Please Clint, sit down. I'll make coffee then we'll have a piece of pie."

"Tess, I don't mean to pry into something that is none of my business, but I sure would like to know what this is all about?"

"Wait till the coffee is done, then I 'll tell you."

As Tess was making coffee standing sideways from Clint, he looked at her fully for the first time. She wasn't very tall, five foot four to five inches at the most, slender and filled out just where a girl should be filled out. Her hair was dark brown, much like his own and came to just below her shoulders. It was pulled back, gathered and tied with a small piece of ribbon. She was wearing jeans, a checkered shirt and boots And she was attractive, darn attractive.

"How long have you been living out here Tess?"

"All my life and alone ever since dad was gunned down."

"Your father was gunned down?"

"He was killed by one of Carter's men who claimed that dad drew on him. That was an out and out lie. After dad was shot I went into Sheridan to get the Marshal. Carter had been there ahead of me. He told the marshal that his man who killed dad shot in self defense and since dad started his draw first, the man was in his rights to defend himself. And that was that."

"But why would Carter have your father killed and why are they trying to do such awful things to you?"

Richard H. Waltner

"Aaron Carter wants my land. More precise, he wants the water on my land and he won't stop until he gets it."

"That means getting rid of you."

Tess looked out he window at the Bighorns which at their higher elevations were still heavily covered with snow. Her fields were green and the sun was shining brightly. It made for a beautiful picture. With tears in her eyes she finally answered Clint.

"Yes Clint, it means getting rid of me and he will succeed. It's only a matter of time."

"Are there none of your neighbors who will help you fight Carter?"

"They're just as frightened as I am. Once I'm out of the way their land is next."

"My lord, how much land does the man want?"

"The entire valley."

Clint was quiet. "Your pie is darn good Tess."

"That's because I'm a pretty darn good cook. Thank you."

"Who helps you run your operation?"

"No one, I do what I can by myself."

"You're not serious, are you?"

"I am Clint, I can hardly look after the cattle I have left."

"What you have left?"

"Yes, Carter and his men have rustled just about half of my herd."

"And the Marshall does nothing?"

"Of course not, he's on Carter's payroll."

"And you've been out here all alone doing your best to fight off those S.O.Bs?"

"Clint, please don't curse. I'm not used to such language."

"Neither am I Tess, but there are times when it's warranted."

"Tess smiled and said, "I guess you're right."

She got to her feet, looked up at Clint and said, "Come with me, but before we go, just how tall are you Clint?"

"Just a bit under six feet two inches."

"You look like you're all muscle. I'll bet you're strong as an ox."

Clint laughed and replied, "Strong as an ox no, but I can hold my own."

Tess led the way to a small fenced in area.

"This is mother's grave. She died first, took ill suddenly and was gone in a matter of days. There was no chance for me to prepare myself for her death."

"That's how my mother went Tess. She died so sudden like. I wasn't even aware she was sick."

"I'm sorry Clint."

"And I'm sorry too Tess."

"And this is Dad's grave. I have no brothers or sisters so I guess that makes me an orphan. I guess not, I'm a bit old to be an orphan."

Clint was silent. After a few moments he said, "That makes two of us Tess. It amazes me how similar we are. My father was a deputy sheriff, he was killed by a drunken drifter when I was five. Mother died some years later and that made me an orphan."

Again Clint was quiet for a time before he spoke. "What kind of animals does this Carter hire anyway that they would come over here with the intent of rapeing you?"

"You saw them and you heard them."

"I believe I'll have to stop in and see that marshal when I go through Sheridan."

"My entire family is buried here Clint. Perhaps you didn't notice, but I have a large piece of paper tacked up behind the back door asking the Carters to please bury me with my family."

Tess pointed to an undisturbed area. "This is where I want to be buried."

"Tess, that's awful. You're planning for your own death? How old are you anyway?"

"With a sad smile on her face Tess Replied. "You've been around long enough to know that's one question you don't ask a woman, but since you did, I'm 23 Clint."

"So am I. Here you are 23 just starting life like I am and already your planning for your death."

"Don't you see, I have to. I'm the only one standing between Carter and my ranch. With me out of the way it will be his. The sheriff will hold a sale, he'll ask for closed bids and claim Carter bid the highest. The only money that will change hands is what Carter pays the sheriff.

"That filthy S.O.B."

"Clint, please."

"Sorry Tess."

"Let's walk to the house I'm sure you can drink another cup of coffee before you leave."

When Clint finished his coffee, he stood, thanked Tess for her kindness and started for the door.

"You don't have to thank me Clint, it is I who thank you. You saved me from being raped by four filthy animals and you saved my life, at least for a little while. And Clint, please forgive me my ill mannered rudeness. I am so sorry for the way I treated you. I'm really not that kind of person."

"For what, just to have them come back later to rape you or kill you or both?"

Clint stepped toward the door, then stopped, turned and faced Tess.

"Tess, I can't leave you. I won't leave you. I'll unload my gear in the barn and find a spot where I can sleep. I'll unroll my bedroll and that will be my bedroom for as long as I'm here. You aren't going to fight Carter and his gang alone any longer."

"Clint, this isn't your fight, please don't make it so. Get on your way before Carter's men return."

"Sorry Tess, but now it's my fight too. What kind of man would I be if I ran off and let a 23 year old girl fight a flock of vultures alone? When they come back, you know darn well what they will do to you. They'll finish what they came for in the first place."

"Yes, I imagine they will."

"Well, change that kind of thinking Tess. If you are raped and killed it will be over my dead body."

"Please Clint, it's not your fight. I don't want you to get hurt."

Clint was quiet, then replied, "Do you really want me to leave Tess?"

"No, no, I'm wearied of living in fear. I'm so tired of being alone."

"Well, you're not alone any longer Tess. Is it OK if I put Lady in the barn?

I want to get her out of the sun. She needs a good rubdown. I'll find a sheltered spot and lay out my bedroll."

"No way Clint, if you insist on staying, there's a bedroom just waiting for you. And Clint, I can't tell you how glad I am that you're staying. Clint smiled and said, "Are you sure Tess. I've been on the trail a long time. Do you think you can trust me?"

Tess laughed and replied, "Well, if I'm going to be raped I'd much sooner it be by you than Carter's filthy men. I'm only kidding Clint, I trust you implicitly."

Clint put Lady in the barn, gave her a good rub-down, put hay in the manger in front of her, covered his saddle with the blanket he used for Lady and himself, picked up his saddle bags and rifle and walked back to the house. Tess was waiting for him. She was smiling and her face had softened.

"Follow me."

Tess led him to a comfortable bedroom at the far end of the house.

"This is where you'll bunk, not in a dusty, musty old barn."

After Clint stored his gear he took Ben's pistol and returned to the kitchen.

"What are you going to do Clint, shoot me?," Tess said with a smile.

"The gun on my hip was dad's Colt. The gun in my hand was given to me by a very dear friend, which I now prefer."

"I never thought I would say a gun looks beautiful, but yours sure does."

"It's almost too nice to carry Tess, but I'm just a bit faster on the draw with it."

Tess was silent, then said, "Clint, you're not a gun fighter, are you?"

"I'm very fast on the draw Tess, but only once have I drawn on a man I intended to kill and he deserved to die because his intention was to kill me, but no, I didn't shoot him."

"So now you're strapping on the gun that you can draw the fastest. Is it me whose going to make a gun fighter out of you?"

"If it comes to that Tess, I will become the gun fighter. You aren't going to make me one."

"Most likely you will be defending me."

"Tess, I can't think of a more justifiable situation under which to become a gun fighter. Now lets sit at the table and talk."

"Clint, you said you got that fancy pistol from a dear friend. Who is he?"

"He was a gun fighter, one of the best, if he hadn't been he wouldn't have been around to give me his pistol. He's no longer living, but after mother died he was like family to me. His name was Raif Sampson, but I called him Ben."

"Tell me about him, will you?"

Once again Clint told the story about meeting Ben and how it was he became such a dear friend. When he finished Tess said, "That's quite a story Clint, I wish I would have had a chance to know Ben. He sounds like a gun fighter with a conscience."

"He was Tess. That became apparent when, after giving me his pistol and teaching me how to use it, he told me to draw it from it's holster only when I have to and when I do, don't hesitate to shoot. Ben was not a man running around looking for men on whom to prove his prowess with a gun."

"May I ask one more question?"

"Sure, fire away."

"How did Ben become such a fast draw with a gun?"

"Ben was born and spent his early teens years in Dakota Territory. His father owned a farm near a military fort. One day he was walking on a trail near the fort and found a pistol, an 1860 Army Colt, which is a front end loader. It must have fallen out of the holster of one of the troopers. I don't suppose that means anything to you."

"No it doesn't."

"Some day I'll explain it to you. Instead of returning it to the fort he kept it. He decided he would become the fastest gun in the west, which would be darn hard to do with that particular revolver. Remember, he was only a kid. He practiced and practiced and when the new Colts came out holding encased cartridges, like my pistol, and like the cartridges in my belt, he purchased one and practiced some more. By now he was no longer a kid, but a young man. He continued practicing until he reached his goal There's little doubt that Ben was the fastest gun in the west. He must have been since he had many gun fights, but didn't die from a bullet."

"Did he ever tell you how many men he killed?"

"No he didn't and I didn't ask him. Now, can we talk ranching and rustling business? First question I have for you is where are your cattle, I don't see any?"

"If you look to the west you'll see a prominent ridge, my herd is below that ridge."

"There's plenty of green grass up here, could they be moved closer to the house so we can keep our eyes on them?"

"They could, however, the Carter's have cut my fences in a dozen different places. There is no way of holding them up here"

"Fences can be repaired. Do you have the necessary supplies?"

"Yes I do."

"I'll get started on repairing them this afternoon."

"I'll help you Clint."

"I'd like that Tess."

The next few days were spent repairing fence. The damage wasn't as bad as Tess had thought. Once the repairs were made they drove the herd to the pastures closer to the house.

One evening after the fence had been repaired and the cattle moved, the two of them were sitting on the back porch admiring the view of the Bighorn Mountains.

"I love this place Clint. There are times when they are just fantastic. This is one of those times. If it weren't for the Carters, it would be idyllic."

"Try not to think of them Tess. Why dampen a perfectly good evening."

Clint turned to face Tess.

"Tess, I, I—"

"What is it Clint?"

"Tess, you are such a pretty girl, the kind of girl a man would want to cozy up to. I'm afraid I get thoughts I shouldn't be. Darn it Tess, you make it difficult for me to behave myself."

"You're not thinking about doing something drastic to me, are you?" Tess said with a coy smile Clint smiled and replied, "Drastic, of course not, natural, I'm afraid so."

"Don't you think we'd be rushing it a bit? We've only known each other a little over two weeks."

"I suppose so, but darn it Tess, what am I supposed to do.? With you so close and so pretty and with such an enticing body and throw in the hard work and beauty of the outdoors and well, it's just about making a wreck of me."

"Well, OK Clinton, if it's that bad I guess we had better take care of it."

"You just said it's too soon."

"It's a girl's prerogative to change her mind, isn't it? Keep in mind Clint, that girls get fired up too. I should tell you one thing however, I'm a virgin so I've had no experience. This will be breaking new ground for me."

"I'm no virgin Tess, but I certainly haven't had much experience. Let's say we break new ground together."

"I say let's do it."

"Are you sure?"

"Let me ask you Clint, isn't it natural for a good looking guy and a pretty girl who have come to know each other real well to want to have sex with each other?"

"Darn right it is. Tess, you're a girl ahead of the times. Most girls would be aghast at the slightest mention of sex."

"I'm not like most girls, Clint. I've had to grow up in a hurry and the beauty and fresh air do things to me too."

"OK," said Clint, "it's time to do away with talk."

He stood, scooped up Tess and carried her into her bedroom.

"I know I don't have to say this Clint, but you will be gentle with me, won't you?"

"Sweetheart, if I may call you that, have I been anything but gentle with you in my talk and actions, other than when we first met?"

"Please don't remind me of that. You always have been gentle with me and you sure can call me Sweetheart. No man has ever called me that. Can I call you Darling?"

"You had better."

"And we can switch if we want to, right?"

"Right. Now Girl, we're getting caught up with talk again. Are we going to get to it or not?"

"Let me tell you Darling, there's no way I could back out now."

For two amateurs their lovemaking was ever so slow and easy. Clint heard a moan from Tess and felt her arms squeeze him tight and he knew.

Tess was the first to speak.

"Clint, you are a man in every way. That was wonderful. I can truthfully say I have never felt such pleasure. I literally got carried away. I don't know why we're so slow in saying it, but I want you to know that I love you."

"And you my love, are every inch a woman."

"Excuse me Clinton," Tess said with a laugh, "But just how do you mean that?"

"Every way it applies Sweetheart. The first time and only time I had sex, other than now, It was hurried and I was under pressure to get it over with.

Afterwards I thought, so what's the big deal? Now Sweetheart, you have shown me what the big deal is and I'm going to want to experience it again and again."

"Me too." Tess was quiet for a moment then asked, "Clint, what do you think is going to happen?"

"You mean with Carter?"

"He's going to come after me. Of that I have no doubt. Not Carter himself, but for sure his men and maybe even a hired gun."

"Tess, I think We'll find out what he's up to next pretty soon."

"Do we have a chance?"

"Of course we do, we always have a chance."

"Just when I've found you and happiness, I don't want to lose it, I don't want to die. I want to live. There's so much to live for. It's wonderful being in love. We can really start to appreciate and enjoy our rich grassland. If it weren't for Carter we could make plans for the future. As it is now, there may not be a future for us."

"Don't give in yet Tess. We'll know better once we find out what he has up his sleeve. By the way, when you mentioned the rich grassland you said our grassland, you meant your grassland, right?"

"Wrong, everything is now ours."

"That doesn't sound right Tess, this is all yours."

"Not any longer, it's ours."

"Clint, may ask I you another question regarding us?"

"Fire away."

"When this issue is resolved and if we're still alive, what are your plans?

You were dead set on going to Montana Territory. Is that still in your plans?"

"Sweetheart, I've come to the conclusion I will not be going to Montana. If you really mean this is ours, this is where I want to stay. Plans?

A soon as we can, we're going into Sheridan and we're going to get married."

"I was so hoping you would say that Clint."

"I've found my girl and there s no way I'm going to give her up."

"We may not have to ride into Sheridan to get married." Reverend Marty, who is kind of like the circuit riding ministers of old, comes out this way quite regularly just to visit with the ranchers and help them with any spiritual issues they may have. So far he has not failed to stop and see me.

I know he would be most happy to marry us. Each time he comes he tells me, 'Tess, you shouldn't be out here alone, you need a man. Every woman needs a man and every man needs a woman. The Good Book says it is not good for man to live alone and that goes for women too.' He hasn't been here for awhile so he's about due. If we have to die, I want for us to be married first."

"Tess, stop thinking we're going to die. We're alive and well now, aren't we? You and I just did a wonderful thing and now you're kind of putting a damper on it."

"I am, aren't I. Alright Mr. Haugen, we can remedy that right now. If, that is, you're game.?"

"Me game?" Clint said with a big smile on his face, "Come on girl, I've had my kicks for the time being. Lets go get a cup of coffee."

"I can't believe what I'm hearing. Coffee instead of me?"

Clint replied with a laugh, "I knew that would get a rise out of you.

Come here you sexy girl, I don't need coffee, I need you."

One noon, after they had been riding all morning they were taking a break.

"Tess my girl," Clint said, "I love being a cowboy. Of course your companionship and the setting increases the joy of it. The grass is so lush and green and the mountains stand as sentinels over your land. I'll tell you one thing, if I were cowboying between Casper and Buffalo I don't think I would enjoy it nearly as much."

"I'm so glad you like it Clint. I'm so glad there's something to hold you here."

"Now, if I were cowboying between Casper and Buffalo and I had you, I would enjoy cowboying there too."

"In other words, I make the big difference."

"The big, big difference Sweetheart."

"I'm so glad to hear that. How wonderful it is knowing I'm loved and by the man I love. Clint you made one big mistake just a short time ago when you were waxing so poetic about the mountains standing as sentinels over the land, You said the Bighorns were guarding my land. It's our land Darling, our land, get it?"

"I will eventually. It takes a shift in thinking, but I promise you I'll get there."

"Clint look up at the mountains, at our fields all around us, at the deep blue sky, doesn't all of it stir something in you?"

"What really stirs something in me is the girl I'm sitting beside."

"Do you think we dare doing it out here?"

"There's no one around for miles. Of course we can make love out here. There are places other than a bedroom you know."

"Of course I know, I'm the one who suggested it."

"Kind of looks to me like we're falling into the same old routine we always do when we're about to make love, we talk too much."

"You're right. It's time for action and not talk."

Later as they were heading back to the house, Tess said, "Wasn't that wonderful Clint. What a setting within which to make love. And you're so right, open fields came along a long time before bed rooms did."

"Clint laughed and said, "You're quite a gal you know, you come up with some pretty funny things once in awhile."

Tess was looking in the direction of Carter's ranch. For a moment she was silent, then she said in a much more somber voice, "I wonder what Carter is dreaming up now?"

"I have a hunch we'll soon find out Tess. It's been three months since the last visit from his henchmen."

"Oh Clint, are we ever going to get out from under this nightmare?"

At first Clint was quiet. Then he answered Tess. "I hate to say this Tess, but I'm afraid it won't end until I kill a few men."

"Oh Clint, no."

"I don't see it any other way."

Now both were deep in thought.

"Are you ready for that Clint?"

"Yes, I am. Ben once told me, 'Clint there will come a time when you'll run into men who deserve killing. Remember, when that time comes, don't hesitate for if you do you'll be the one who ends up dead.'

Before I had only myself to look after, now I have you. No one will lay a hand on you unless it's over my dead body."

"You mean that don't you? That Ben, he must have been quite a man."

"He was Tess. I'm so lucky that he accepted me as a friend and took me into his confidence. And yes, I mean every word of it. The Good Book says 'till death do us part, and that's the only thing that's going to separate us. Now let's forget about Carter and enjoy this beautiful day."

For awhile Tess was quiet as they rode along. Then she said softly, "You could get killed Clint and then Carter's men would kill me."

"That's a possibility, but I'll tell you one thing if they get me down I'll last long enough to kill them all. Then you skedaddle out of here and go to Sheridan just as fast as you can."

"No Clint, I would never abandon you."

"I'll be dead Tess."

"So will I."

"Alright, enough of this dying and being dead talk. Look around you Tess, it's just so great to be alive."

As they rode through Tess' herd of cattle they counted 125 head.

"I had 250 head, Carter rustled half of my herd."

"Some day we'll get them back."

There were frequent rains and the country side got even more beautiful.

It was a few weeks later when they had another visit from Carter's men. Clint was in the back of the house building a chute for the day when they would drive cattle to market. He looked up and saw a cloud of dust approaching. He ran into the house and into the bedroom returning with Ben's Colt. He opened the gate of the Colt, put it on half cock, pulled a single cartridge from his belt and put it into the cylinder.

Tess was watching.

"Only one cartridge Clint? There must be several men."

"No Sweetheart, there were already five cartridges in the cylinder.

Usually one of the chambers is left unloaded so the hammer doesn't rest on a loaded cartridge. Should the gun be dropped and it lands on the hammer it would most likely discharge, perhaps killing the owner or someone else near bye."

As the riders approached they could count six men. Tess immediately broke into tears.

"Six men, you won't have a chance. Oh Clint, is this the end?"

"I don't think so Sweetheart. I have a plan. No one is going to outdraw me. Don't count me out yet."

The rider's pulled up in front of the house. The man Clint beat on their last visit called out, "Come on out Haugen."

Clint looked out the window. The men had their guns holstered. He quickly stepped outside.

"Six of you, you don't give me very good odds do you?"

Then he noticed that all of men were leaning on the saddle horn in front of them.

"Well, is it to be a gunfight or not."

"No gun fight." It was an elderly man who spoke up. "After we started out from Carter's, we stopped and had a conference. Carter always has someone do his dirty work. Well, we're sick and tired of being the ones.

We have hurt more people in many ways than we care to admit. We decided no more, enough is enough. You don't have to go for your gun. We don't intend to harm either you or Tess. Further, we are well aware that if you have to go for your gun, several of us are going to be dead and none of us is anxious to die. We most likely will get you, but at too damn high a price. We're leaving Carter and we're leaving the Valley."

"Are you boys serious?"

"Damn right we are. I said that enough is enough."

"I'm glad you decided not to make me draw boys, Reif told me in no uncertain terms; 'Clint, if you have to draw, you have to kill. If you don't you're the one who will end up dead.' If just one of you had drawn I would have had to empty my gun."

There was silence for a moment. Clint was still poised to draw, not quite ready to believe what the elderly man had said. Then he spoke up.

"Did I hear you mention the name Reif?"

"That's something that just slipped out of my mouth."

"No, seriously, did you mention the name Reif?"

"Well, if you have to know I did."

"That's not a very common name. You weren't by chance refering to Reif Sampson.?

Clint was shocked. He was silent then answered.

"As a matter of fact I was. Do you know Reif Sampson?"

"Know him, He was my old card playing buddy back in Santa Fe. In fact Reif and I were darn good friends. How did you come to know Reif?"

"Well, you certainly have the geography right. I came up from Santa Fe in spring. To answer your question, Reif was my neighbor and once we became friends, he literally adopted me. I knew Reif since I was 10 years old."

"I can't believe it. You know Reif Sampson."

"I sure did. Reif died about 5 years ago. Do you remember the Colt Reif carried."

"I sure am sorry to hear that Reif is no longer living. Although we haven't been together for many a year, I've lost a good friend. Yes, I remember Reif's Colt. It was the most beautiful revolver I ever saw. The entire gun was engraved and it had the most beautiful blue job and Gold inlays on either side. Reif had that revolver especially made for him at the Colt factory. I needn't tell you it cost him a small fortune."

"I'm going to turn ever so much to my side so you can see the top part of the Colt above my holster. See if you can recognize the gun."

Clint turned ever so slightly. The elderly man looked and looked again.

"Yes, yes, that's Reif's gun. How in the world did you come by it?"

"Reif knew his gun slinging days were over and that he didn't have much time left to live. One evening we were visiting and he handed me this here pistol. I didn't want to take his Colt, but he insisted. You see, Reif had no kin. Well, he didn't have to argue with me. Not only did he give me his Colt, he taught me how to draw it and shoot. I trained and trained until Reif said I was actually faster than he was. There isn't a day that goes bye that I don't practice some."

"Reif said you are faster than he?"

"He sure did."

"Lord, had we drawn on you, you might have killed us all."

"That was my thinking, Mr. Mr—"

"My name's Wade Folsome."

"When Reif died, I lost my best friend ever. He didn't tell me his name until he lay on the floor dying. His ticker just gave out. I called him Ben and that suited him fine. In fact, when thinking about him, I think about Ben, not Reif."

"Now I know for sure you knew Reif. We knew each other for quite a spell before he told me his real name. I called him Charlie. Mr. Haugen, I'm damn sorry we caused you so much trouble. Had I only known, I just might have put a bullet in Carter."

"My name's Clint. The one you should be apologizing to is the girl I love, Tess Hawks. She's the one who had to bear the brunt of Carter's evilness."

"Call her out, will you Clint?"

"Tess, would you step out here?"

Tess stepped out with a look of amazement on her face. By now she expected several men would be lying dead on the ground. Instead all she heard was talk.

"Miss Hawks, I want to apologize for all the grief the boys and myself caused you. I truly am sorry. I just discovered that Clint's friend Ben, was my very dear friend and card playing buddy, Rief Sampson. Had I only known. Lord, I am so sorry. Ma'am, the boys and I have left Carter and are leaving the valley heading for Dakota Territory You will never get any more trouble from us."

"Mr., Mr.—"

"As I told Clint, my name is Charlie Folsome."

"Mr. Folsome, I've looked over the men and I don't see the man who killed my father. Where is he?"

"One of Carter's men killed your father? He done it because he wanted your land, right?"

"And my water."

"Ma'am, that must have happened before I joined Carter's crew."

One of the other men spoke up.

"That was Clyde Patrick. It might give you some satisfaction Ma'am to know he was killed in a shoot out in Buffalo."

"It doesn't bring my father back to me, but yes, it does give me a bit of satisfaction to know he died the way my dad died."

"Well Clint and Tess, the boys and I are going to mosey on now. We've left Carter and now we're leaving the valley Clint, the odds are much more even now. Oh, by the way, where is Reif buried?"

"In the Santa Fe cemetery, his grave is up in the northwest corner. I had a marker put up with his name on it. It reads Reif (Ben) Sampson. If you get back to Santa Fe and want to look up his grave site, you can't miss it."

"Reif (Ben) Sampson, I'll bet he got a chuckle out of that."

"As a matter of fact he did. He forced a smile then told me, 'Clint if you want to include Ben in my name, go right ahead and do it."

"Goodbye Clint and Tess. Clint I hope you have a chance at that damn Carter."

THE CHALLENGE

As they turned to leave, the youngest of the men said, "Mr. Haugen, my name's Cody, there's something I must tell you. Carter said that if the six of us couldn't fix things, he was going to send to Cheyenne for a fast gun."

Clint smiled, then said, "Thanks Cody, looks like I'll be able to put Ben's advice to work after all."

The man who had knocked Tess down spoke up, "Miss Tess, I want to apologize for hitting you, for threatening to rape you and for scaring you half to death. I promise you, I've turned over a new leaf. Can you forgive me? And Mr. Haugen, I'm glad you gave me such a beating, I had it coming and it sure knocked some sense into my head. When we got back to Carter's, I got to thinking, me a big man, a big bully and I hit you Miss Tess. None of us would have raped you. That wasn't in our plans, rough you up a bit and scare you, but not rape you. That was Carter's idea."

"What's your name?" asked Tess.

"It's Clayton, but everyone calls me Clay."

"Well Clay, it's a bit hard for me to do, but I forgive you. The way things have turned out there must have been some purpose for all that has happened."

"Thank you Miss Tess, I feel better now."

The men turned their horses, waved and were gone.

Tess looked up into Clint's face with tear streaked cheeks and said, "Clint, the Lord sure does move in strange and mysterious ways, doesn't He."

"He sure does Sweetheart."

It wasn'smore than a week later that Reverend Marty, the traveling Preacher, stopped in to see Tess. He was surprised to see Clint and Tess living together.

"Tell me," he asked, have the two of you been living in sin?"

Tess started stammering then Clint took over.

"Well Reverend, if you want to call it that, but no more so than our forefathers did when they moved from the eastern seaboard into the wilderness. As I'm sure you know, many of those couples started living together because there was no minister around to marry them. However, when a circuit riding minister did show up, he married them. The situation is the same with Tess and I. There has been no one out here to Marry us until you showed up."

"I never thought of it that way Clint, but you're right. why didn't you ride into Sheridan and get married?"

"We couldn't leave the place Reverend, there's been too much trouble with old man Carter. He already has run off with half of Tess' herd."

"Yes, I've been hearing bad things about Aaron. In fact I stopped there yesterday and didn't receive a very warm welcome."

"I'm surprised you received any welcome at all. Now Reverend, will you marry Tess and I?"

"I will consider it a privelege Mr. Haugen. First of all, how long have you two known each other?"

"I arrived in the valley in late April. It is now the early part of August. I would say about four months."

"I would prefer that you had known each other longer, but since you have already been living in sin for some time, I sure will go ahead and marry you." And he did and when he left, Clint and Tess were husband and wife.

One evening after Carter's men had left, Clint and Tess were sitting on the back step admiring the view.

"Well Sweetheasrt, we have one more challenge standing before us before we can really breathe freely."

"What is it Clint? Carter's men have left him."

"Yes they have, but he told the men that if they couldn't resolve the problem to his satisfaction he was going to send for a gun fighter from Cheyenne. Don't you remember?"

"I don't want to. Clint, will this never end? I can't take anymore. You have no assurance you will be able to outdraw him." Tess broke down and cried, deep sobs came from her lips.

Clint took Tess in his arms and tried to comfort her.

"I will Tess, I have to. I'm going to have to increase time spent each day practicing my draw."

"How long are we going to have to wait for the gunfighter to show up?"

"I have a hunch when Carter finds out his men deserted him, it won't be long at all. Carter is getting desperate."

Two weeks went by and no gun fighter showed up Tess was a bundle of nerves.

"Calm down Tess, he does have to come from Cheyenne you know.

He'll be here soon enough. Let's get up early tomorrow and ride the range, that should help you get Carter and his gun slinger off your mind."

It was another beautiful day. When they stopped for lunch Clint said, "Something is wrong with Lady, Tess. She just isn't her old self. She seems to tire easily and she stumbles quite often, something she has never done."

"She's getting old Clint, just how old is Lady?"

"When I bought her she was either 10 or 12 years old. That would make her 17 or 19 years old."

"That's old for a horse. Just like people, horses get old and eventually die. That's something you're going to have to face."

"She sure has been a faithful horse, she was the best companion a man could have as we came up from Santa Fe. I think I'd better not ride her anymore."

"There are one or two good horses in the pasture. You'll have to cut one out and break her."

"I've never broken a horse Tess."

Tess smiled and said, "You're a cowboy remember, and cowboys break horses. Looks like you're going to get your chance."

"You're so right Sweetheart. I guess I have my work cut out for me. Do you have anything for bruises and sore muscles?"

"Believe it or not, I do."

Trying to break a horse that has never been ridden was no easy task for Clint. He needed the ointment. Gradually he made progress. When he felt the horse was ready to learn who was boss, Tess stood at the gate.

Clint climbed into the saddle. He yelled out, "Open the gate Tess."

Horse and rider literally flew out of the corral. Tess saw them dissapear over a ridge and waited patiently for them to return. It was a full hour before they did. Tess could tell by the smile on Clint' face and the droop of the horse's head that Clint had won.

"She's going to be a good horse Tess, now that she knows who's boss."

Clint rode her every day. When he swung onto the saddle she no longer tried to buck him off.

"Well Tess my girl, have I proven I'm a cowboy as well as a fast draw with a gun?"

"You have proven you're a first class cowboy Clint."

It wasn't a week later that Clint went to the barn to give Lady hay. She was lying on her side and breathing heavily.

"Lady's down Tess. My faithful Lady is dying and I can't help her. She was my constant companion for a couple of years when we came north.

She never let me down. We got caught in a freak snow storm. The wind was strong, it was snowing and cold and I could see no shelter of any kind. I thought for sure I would freeze to death. Sensing my problem, she knelt down and provided me with some shelter when I laid tightly up against her. You now Sweetheart, horses aren't supposed to stay down very long, but she stayed right where she was till morning by which time the storm had blown itself out. Only then did she stand. All through the night she kept snickering to let me know she was with me. Tess, would you think I'm crazy if I slept with Lady tonight? I know she won't make it through the night and I don't want her to die alone."

"Of course I don't think you're crazy. I want you to be with Lady when she dies. My poor darling you've lost so much. First your dad, then your mother, then Ben and now your Lady."

"Yes Sweetheart, I've lost a lot, but look what I've found."

Clint took Tess into his arms, looked into her face and said, "My Sweetheart, my wonderful wife. Just look at what I've found. Do you know that Ben told me I was going to find you? When he lay dying he told me I was such a good boy, being friendly and looking after a lonely old gun fighter who could no longer take care of himself. He made me promise to always be a kind, careing and gentle man. This man who taught me to perhaps be the fastest gun in the west, told me never to stop being a gentle and caring person. Then he said, 'Clint, there is a beautiful young woman out there somewhere and she's waiting for you.

You're going to find her in a way you can't anticipate. Just keep looking for her.' He was so right Tess, I've found her and I've never been so happy."

"Hold me Clint, just hold me tight. I too was looking for you, but I almost gave up hope of ever finding you. I thought I would surely die.

And to think, I held a gun on you and almost drove you away from me."

Tess broke down in tears, "I'm so sorry my dear husband, so sorry."

"Sweetheart, the way we met each other was meant to be. I don't believe for a moment that when I came down off that high ridge to the east looking for water for Lady and myself that I came to your place by accident. Look what might have happened if I had not come. It all played out the way God planned it. Ben was so right."

"Let me get you a blanket Clint, it's likely to be pretty cool in the barn. You go out and stay with Lady."

Shortly after Tess got up in the morning Clint came into the house. Tears were in his eyes.

"Well Tess, Lady is gone. She died at around 2:30 this morning. She knew I was with her. She snickered off and on like she always did and she would move her nose just to touch me. Then she became quiet and I knew she was gone."

Clint walked to the back door, opened it and gazed across the valley to the Bighorns. Tess clould see he was weeping. His sholders were shaking. She came up behind him, put her arms around his waist and lay her head against his shoulder.

"I'm sorry Darling, so sorry. You've lost a faithful friend. We both know how painful that can be. What are you going to do with Lady?"

"I'm going to go a little ways beyond the family cemetery and bury her there. I'll tell you one thing. I'm not going to drag her behind a hill and leave her for the vultures to peck out her eyes and the wolves and coyotes to tear the flesh from her bones."

"That's going to take a pretty big hole Clint."

"Yes, and I'm going to have to get started. I'll hitch up the team, tie a rope in front of her back legs and one up high behind her frontlegs then carefully have the team pull her to the hole. I'll manuvere them in such a way that they can pull her into the hole. By evening Lady will be buried."

Clint turned to face Tess.

"I'm sorry Tess, I'm not being much of a man, but I can't help it. It will pass."

"Clint, didn't Ben say you were a gentle man and you should not change? I would be surprised if you didn't shed a few tears. I think you picked a good place for Lady's grave: When we sit on the back porch and look across the valley to the Bighorns, we will be looking over Lady's grave."

Clint was right, by evening Lady was buried and the earth over her grave was smoothed. He took a piece of heavy planking and with chisel and hammer inscribed, HERE LIES LADY, FAITHFUL FRIEND AND COMPANION. Next he secured it to a post and drove it deep into the ground.

The Fastest Gun
In The Territories

And then they came. Clint was fixing the gate into the corral when he looked up. Three men were coming from the south. They didn't seem to be in a hurry.

"That," he said, "Is a sign of confidence. We'll see."

He hurried into the house, went directly to the bedroom and came out with Ben's pistol and belt.

"What is it Clint?" Tess asked.

"The time has arrived Tess. The gun slinger along with two other men are coming up the road."

Tess immediately broke into tears.

"Oh Clint, I'm so scared. I don't want to lose you. I can't go on without you."

"Aren't you being a bit premature Tess? I'm not dead yet."

Clint spun the cylinder of Ben's Colt. All six chambers were loaded. He removed his dad's pistol belt and replaced it with Ben's.

"Tess, look out the window and see if you recognize any of the men."

"It's Aaron Carter, I'd know him anywhere. The other men I don't know. It isn't hard to tell who the gun slinger is, he rides his horse as if he owns the world."

"Most likely he thinks he does, Tess."

Clint looked carefully at the position of the three men. He wanted to know exactly where all three were positioned. The gunman was directly in front of the door, Old man Carter would be to his left and slightly behind him, but not out of his peripheral vision. The third man was directly left of the gunman far enough away that he wouldn't get hit by any stray slugs.

Clint took Tess into his arms.

"Sweetheart," he said, "This long ordeal is about over."

"Oh Clint, I'm so scared."

Clint smiled and said, "Whatever you do, don't stand directly behind the door. Look at my hands, not a tremor. I'm ready for him Sweetheart."

He opened the door, stepped outside and descended the steps. He was facing the gunman.

"So, you're Clint Haugen and you're supposed to be a fast gun. With a name like Haugen that strikes me as being a bit funny. I like going up against a man with a name. Say, that's a fancy gun you have in your holster. Sorry to tell you Haugen, but soon it will be mine."

Clint readied himself, there wasn't the slightest tremor in his hands.

"You are a cocksure S.O.B. You talk too much."

He saw the man's gun hand move. Clint's first slug hit him in the center of his chest. The man staggered. His pistol was out of it's holster, but the barrel was pointing towards the ground. Clint's second bullet hit him again in the center of the chest. He took a step backward, but the gunman was still struggling to bring up his gun. Clint took deliberate aim and shot the gunman between his eyes. He fell forward on his face and didn't so much as move a muscle. Clint walked forward, his gun at the ready, he reached down and picked up the dead man's gun and threw it toward the porch.

Tess had stepped out on the porch. Suddenly she screamed out, "Clint behind you."

Clint swung his gun under his left arm and fired. At the same time he felt a heavy blow on his left shoulder. He shifted his position just a bit and put a bullet through Aaron Carter's head. Carter fell forward, his head resting on his horse's neck. Clint holstered his pistol then fell on his knees, his head hanging down. In a moment Tess was by his side.

"Clint, oh Clint my Darling," she sobbed, "you're hurt."

Clint looked up at Tess and with a strained smile said, "Thanks for keeping your eyes on him Sweetheart. I guess I was so focused on the gunslinger that for a moment I forgot about Carter. Had you not screamed when you did, I'm afraid I'd be lying on the ground, dead like the gunslinger. Carter must have been aiming to shoot me in the head.

My first shot must have startled him just enough that his gun shifted slightly.

I'm hit in the shoulder Tess, nothing more. I guess I'm a pretty tough bird, hard to kill. It's over Darling, no more will you have to live in fear."

"Oh thank You God and thank you Ben."

Clint saw movement from the third man and immediately his gun was in his hand.

"Don't shoot. I'm unarmed."

"Come closer."

The man walked up to Tess and Clint. Clint looked him over carefully, then slid his pistol back into it's holster.

"Let me look at that shoulder."

"I'm going to turn it a bit and it's going to hurt. I want to see if any bones are broken."

He twisted Clint's arm. Clint let out a yell. The stranger was satisfied no bones were broken.

"The bullet must be lying next to a bone, it will have to be removed."

Tess repeated herself.

"Oh thank You God, and thank you Ben."

Then she said in obvious surprise, "Amon, is that you?"

"You're Tess Hawks, aren't you? I heard the name Tess mentioned a number of times at the ranch, but had no idea it was you. Isn't this the place where your folks lived?"

"I am Amon, only my name is Tess Haugen now and yes this is Dad's Homestead."

"I figured it was when the gunman called out your husband's name."

"We were in school together for one year. I was in the first grade And Amon you must have been in the eighth. Clint, this is Amon Carter. Amon are you a doctor?"

"Yes Tess, I am, and you Tess were the cute button of a girl with braids with which you were forever fussing."

"I hated those braids."

Clint extended his right hand to Amon. Amon took it. Then Clint said, "I'm sorry Dr. Carter, but your father left me no other choice but to kill him."

Amon was quiet for a moment.

"Mr Haugen—"

"It's Clint."

"Clint, it's for the best. My father and I were estranged. We never communicated. At times I forgot I had a father. He was mentally sick.

From what I've been told, he was a very dangerous man. All he thought about was land and money. He drove ranchers off their land, rustled cattle and even had a couple of ranchers killed just to get their land.

Now that he's out of the picture, there will be peace in this beautiful Valley."

"Dad wasn't always this way Clint. When he was a young man he was an ideal father, but then greed over took him. He had become an evil man, Look what he did to you, he brought a fast gun out from Cheyenne to Kill you. I'm happy he didn't succeed. You have done every person in the valley a great favor. By the way, how did you ever learn to draw so fast? On the way over here dad said the hired killer was the best."

"That's a long story Amon, someday I'll tell you. By the way, why did you accompany your dad and the gunman over here?"

"To do just what I'm about to do, take care of any bullet wounds."

"Amon," Tess spoke up, "My dad was one of the men your father had killed."

"Oh Tess, No. When was that."

"Well over a year ago. He wanted our land, but even more he wanted the water on our land. He thought that by bringing a gun slinger out here he would get what he wanted. Instead he's dead. If Clint were killed, I have no doubt that I would also have been killed."

"I'm so sorry Tess. I wish I could undo all of his wrongs, but that's not possible."

"Amon please, in no way do I blame you."

Amon walked over to the fallen gun slinger, then to his father. Next he walked to his horse and took a small satchel out of his saddle bags. Then he returned to where Clint and Tess were still kneeling on the ground.

"Well," he said, "There's no help for either of them. Their killing days are over. Can we go inside, I have to remove that bullet."

With a probe and a forceps, by turning and twisting he was able to remove the bullet from Clint's shoulder.

Clint let out a yell and nearly passed out.

"There, it's out. Tess, do you have some whiskey?"

"We do Amon."

"Get the bottle of whiskey and pour some of into Clint's wound. Sorry Clint, but this is going to hurt."

Clint let out another yell.

"Clint, if it weren't that you are so muscular, that bullet would have caused considerable damage. I'm not too concerned about infection.

Tess, I want you to boil water, mix it with a pretty good amount of salt, soak a rag with it and put it on Clint's shoulder. Do that a couple of times a day."

"Amon?"

"Yes Tess."

"When did you go to medical college?"

"I left home after school here in the valley and went back east. One thing I must say about dad, which is positive, he wanted me to go to medical school. He paid all my bills."

"Why did you come back to the valley?"

"A couple of dad's neighbors wrote and told me what he was doing.

I'm going to do my best to see if I can't right some of the wrongs dad was responsible for. I had hoped I could talk some sense into him. I was wrong. Clint, you did all of us a favor. You know Tess, it's so good to be back home. I'm going to stay here and take over Dad's operation."

"Are you married Amon?"

"I sure am Tess. I have two daughters. You'll have to come over and meet Sarah and the girls.

"We'd love to Amon."

Clint spoke up.

"Amon, I hate to bring this up now, but since you will be taking over your dad's operation, this is just as good a time as any. Your dad rustled 125 head of Tess' cattle. We would like to have them returned. He branded over Tess' brand, but he wasn't successful in erasing it. When you're settled, I'll show you what the double brand, Tess' and your dad's, look like. Do you have any hands left?"

"Yes, two trusted men with families. I will need a couple more but they will be local boys, all married boys. Of course your cattle will be returned to you. Yours and those belonging to other ranchers as well. I assure you that from now on this is going to be the best valley in all of Wyoming Territory in which to live. Now, I must be going. By the way Clint, I'm not much on guns, but I can't help but admire that pistol of yours. Where did you ever get such a beautiful pistol?"

"That ties in with my ability to draw as fast as lightening. When we get together I'll answer both of your questions.

"I'm looking forward to it."

"Hopefully, from now on till I die, I will be able to retire this beautiful pistol, hang it on the wall and admire it and strap on dad's Colt. Dad was a sheriff in Santa Fe and was shot in the back, killing him. His pistol was given to mom by one of the deputies and she gave it to me. I'm fast with it also, but just a bit faster with Ben's gun, or the fancy pistol. By the way Amon, please don't tell anyone about the shoot out with the dead gunslinger. If word gets out, I fear our valley won't be peaceful for long. Every punk who thinks he's fast with a gun will come looking for me. I really don't think he'll be missed by anyone."

"Rest assured Clint, I won't breath a word of it. You did a good thing by ridding Wyoming of the likes of him. I never saw such arrogance.

Clint, do you think you have enough strength in your right arm to help me turn dad sideways so I can take him home and bury him?"

"No problem Amon, I have a lot of strength in my right arm."

All three walked out to where Aaron was still on the saddle with his head resting on the neck of his horse. Clint stooped down and picked up Aaron's gun.

"Here Amon, you might want to take this with you."

"Keep it Clint and add it to your collection, I have no use for it. I'll send my two hired men over here with a buckboard to bring the body of the dead gunslinger back home. We'll bury him in the hills somewhere."

Looking carefully at the gun Clint said, "Well I'll be darned. It's an 1860 Army Colt just like the one Ben found which started him on his way to being a fast gun. Thanks Amon. Tell you what, I'll take care of that little chore. Your men just might do a little talking, not on purpose of course, but you know how it is. Sometimes we all say things we shouldn't."

"Are you going to need help?"

"I don't think so, but if I do I know someone who will be more than eager to help" Clint answered turning to Tess.

When Aaron was tied securely to the saddle, Amon said "Now don't forget, come pay Sarah, the girls and I a visit."

"We'll be sure to do that."

"Amon, how are you going to explain your father's death and the absence of the gun slinger to your family and hired men? I'll think of something Clint. I could tell them that the gunman wanted more money and when dad refused, he shot dad and then rode off. Something like that."

After Amon left and Tess and Clint were back in the house, Tess threw her arms around Clint, laid her head against his chest and wept a long time. Finally she said, "Darling, there is no question in my mind that you are the fastest gun in the west. I didn't even see your pistol leave it's holster. That dead gunman just cleared his holster when your first bullet hit him. For all practical purposes the fight was over then. You shot him three times."

"I wasn't going to take any chances Tess. I was afraid he might have enough energy left in him to raise his gun. When the second bullet didn't drop him, I knew I had to shoot one more time."

"Yes, right between the eyes. Do you have any regrets?"

"None whatsoever. That man wanted to kill me and perhaps you too.

Tess, a calmness came over me that I never experienced before. I knew I would outdraw the gunslinger."

In a low voice Tess said, "You know why, don't you?"

"Yes Tess, God's hand was steadying mine."

"Now, what are we going to do with his body?"

"We'll load him in the buck board, take him back in the hills and bury him.

I've got only one arm Tess, you're going to have to help me.

"It will be a pleasure Darling."

A Filly Of Our Own

Some weeks later, after their cattle had been returned, Tess and Clint were sitting on the steps of the back porch watching the sunset, Tess with her arm linked through Clint's and her head resting against his shoulder.

They sat in silence for a few minutes then Tess said, "Clint, are you going to stop wearing your gun?"

For a few moments Clint did not respond.

"No Tess, I'm not. A revolver on my side has become a part of me. I'd feel naked without it. I know there is peace in the valley, but there are still rattle snakes, coyotes, wolves, skunks, any number of varmints that we need to get rid of. Further, Clarence told me that this may not be the wild west it once was, but it sure isn't tamed yet. Do you want me to stop wearing my gun?"

"No Clint, I don't. You just wouldn't be Clint Haugen if you didn't have a gun on your hip. I agree, it's become a part of you. Will you be wearing Ben's revolver?"

"No, Ben's revolver will be retired. I have three other Colt's from which to choose, Dad's, Kid Zoro's and the gunslinger's. Old man Carter's 1860 Army Colt is a collection piece, impractical today, but I still want to hang onto it. It's dad's Colt that will be riding on my hip from now on."

"Next time we're in Sheridan I'm going to get a nice piece of oak wood, fancy it all up and have a jeweler take a piece of bronze and inscribe on it, TO MY ADOPTED SON CLINT FROM HIS ADOPTIVE FATHER BEN. I'll put the bronze plate at the top of the oak board then I'll drill holes and put two pegs into it, attach it to the wall and that's where Ben's gun will be retired. Oh, I might strap it on now and then when we go to Sheridan, but that would be the only time."

"Another question Darling? Are you going to keep practicing your fast draw?"

"For the time being, yes. Not as often or as long. Ben told me to never let up, that I would get rusty in a hurry."

"I'm glad Sweetheart. Now my last question. Would you teach me to shoot a revolver?"

"Come on Tess, you're not serious? You're joking with me, aren't you?"

"No Clint, I'm serious. I want you to teach me how to shoot a revolver.

I'm pretty good with my rifle, but I've never shot a revolver."

"I sure will Darling, it will be my pleasure. Tell me, are you going to start carrying one too," Clint said with a smile.

"Well now, I just might do that."

Again there were a few minutes of silence. And again it was Tess who broke it.

"Isn't it wonderful to breathe freely for the first time in, well for me, for the first time in years. Never again will we have to worry about Aaron Carter."

"Yes Sweetheart, we should sleep good from now on. I've been looking at the herd. It needs to be culled, we need to get rid of some of the old stock and replace it with new."

"That will take a couple of new bulls, and Clint we don't have the money at the moment to buy bulls."

Suddenly Clint perked up.

"Yes we do Tess. Didn't I tell you that Ben gave me around $15,000? In fact I have a Bankers Check that should be put in the bank. We have money for bulls and then some."

"How much did you say Clint?"

"Fifteen-thousand dollars."

"That's a fortune Clint. We can do a lot more than just buy bulls, we can do some fixing up around here. I have ideas for the house."

"You wouldn't be a woman if you didn't."

"I'd like to get a couple of young mares, maybe even a stallion and raise a few horses."

"We certainly have the land for both cattle and horses." Looking up at Clint, Tess continued "Now that we're settled on guns, cattle and horses, Isn't it about time we had a little filly of our own.? You're going to need lots of help with all the livestock to tend to."

"You know Sweetheart, it is about time, isn't it?"

"Yes," said Tess. Then looking at Clint she continued with narrowed eyes, "And how about starting on the project right now? There's one thing we have to do before we have that little filly you know. With a good right arm and a sore left arm, do you think you're up to it?"

"Try me Sweetheart, just try me."

Clint leaned over and gave Tess a kiss. It was meant to be a light kiss, but it turned out to be hot and passionate."

Tess stood and said, "Hurry Clint, I don't know if I'll even make it to the bedroom."

"Now that really wouldn't be too bad, would it?"

"Not at all, but I do believe the bed will be just a bit more comfortable."